"I was thinking that even if Mom makes a full recovery from this, I need to start making some plans for her future."

"Nantucket is her home," Jo reminded Daniel.

"I know, but I have to be practical. I'm all she's got, and I have a business to run in the city, not to mention a rebellious teenager to keep an eye on," he said. "Just don't go spending any more than you absolutely have to on this season's crop until I can figure things out, okay?"

"Ella hired me to bring in the crop and that's what I intend to do. If you're suggesting that I not do everything in my power to make sure it's a successful crop, then…"

His eyes blazed as he turned suddenly to face her. "Perhaps I should get someone else," he said.

"Perhaps you should talk to your mother before you go around firing the help she hired," Jo replied tersely before heading back to the bog.

Books by Anna Schmidt

Love Inspired

Caroline and the Preacher
A Mother for Amanda
The Doctor's Miracle
Love Next Door
Matchmaker, Matchmaker…
Lasso Her Heart
Mistletoe Reunion
Home at Last

Love Inspired Historical

Seaside Cinderella
Gift from the Sea

ANNA SCHMIDT

is an award-winning author of more than twenty works of historical and contemporary fiction. She is a two-time finalist for the coveted RITA® Award from Romance Writers of America as well as three times a finalist for a *Romantic Times BOOKreviews* Reviewers' Choice Award. The most recent *Romantic Times BOOKreviews* Reviewers' Choice Nomination was for her 2008 Love Inspired Historical novel, *Seaside Cinderella,* which is the first of a series of four historical novels set on the romantic island of Nantucket. Critics have called Anna "a natural writer, spinning tales reminiscent of old favorites like *Miracle on 34th Street.*" Her characters have been called "realistic" and "endearing" and one reviewer raved, "I love Anna Schmidt's style of writing!"

Home at Last

Anna Schmidt

Steeple
Hill®

Published by Steeple Hill Books™

STEEPLE HILL BOOKS

Steeple
Hill®

Recycling programs
for this product may
not exist in your area.

ISBN-13: 978-0-373-87545-0

HOME AT LAST

Copyright © 2009 by Jo Horne Schmidt

All rights reserved. Except for use in any review, the reproduction
or utilization of this work in whole or in part in any form by any
electronic, mechanical or other means, now known or hereafter
invented, including xerography, photocopying and recording, or in
any information storage or retrieval system, is forbidden without
the written permission of the editorial office, Steeple Hill Books,
233 Broadway, New York, NY 10279 U.S.A.

This is a work of fiction. Names, characters, places and incidents are
either the product of the author's imagination or are used fictitiously, and
any resemblance to actual persons, living or dead, business establishments,
events or locales is entirely coincidental.

This edition published by arrangement with Steeple Hill Books.

® and TM are trademarks of Steeple Hill Books, used under license.
Trademarks indicated with ® are registered in the United States Patent
and Trademark Office, the Canadian Trade Marks Office and in other
countries.

www.SteepleHill.com

Printed in U.S.A.

God is both refuge and strength for us,
A help always ready in trouble.
—*Psalms* 46:1

To all who struggle to make sense of tragedy
as they move forward in love and life.

Chapter One

Daniel Armstrong worked his way through the throngs of guests waiting to check in or out of the Barrington Hotel. *His* hotel—and for the time being, his home. He picked up discarded paper coffee cups from one of the side tables and straightened a lampshade. One of the first things he'd done after taking ownership of the hotel was to tell his staff that service was to be the hotel's byword and that going the extra mile to keep the hotel looking its best would be rewarded in kind.

He put his smile on autopilot and flipped open his cell phone as he edged around a group of teens and their teachers from the United Kingdom sprawled on the floor near the elevators. "Greg? The lobby's beginning to look like a refugee camp. We need to get our guests into rooms. What's going on with housekeeping?"

"I'm on it," his general manager assured him. "Should have the UK group in their rooms within half an hour. Did you get that call?"

"Which one?" Daniel's phone had been vibrating most of the morning.

"Her ladyship," Greg replied.

Daniel groaned. His ex-wife, Gloria, was the only child of Robert Barrington and the heir apparent to the Barringtons' hotel empire and its five locations across Manhattan. The fact that the family no longer owned this particular hotel—that it had been the only property Daniel had walked out of the marriage with—rarely seemed to matter to Gloria. The hotel's location close to Carnegie Hall made it attractive to Gloria for preconcert parties. Besides, it still carried the family name, and she seemed to relish dictating orders to the staff whenever she saw fit.

"I'll call her back. Anything else?"

"Nothing I can't handle."

"Okay. Catching lunch upstairs if you need me."

Daniel took the private elevator to the apartment his ex-father-in-law had constructed on the top floor of the hotel. As such spaces went, this one was more functional than luxurious. A living room, galley kitchen, two bedrooms with connecting bath. It was the wraparound terrace that made the place special. From there Daniel could see Central Park to the north and almost to Times Square to the south. With spring in the air, he'd taken to allowing himself a rare break for lunch on the terrace. The scheduled time-out also provided a measure of calm whenever he had to deal with the mess his private life had become. Daniel headed for the terrace as he dialed Gloria's private number.

"Daniel," she said breathlessly, as if surprised by his call. "How lovely to hear from you."

"You called?"

"Oh, I see we're all business today. Very well. Bottom line—Chef Georges has accepted me into his culinary program, and I leave for Paris tonight."

The very idea of Gloria in a kitchen boggled the mind, but Daniel resisted the urge to antagonize her. Chef Georges was currently the person to see and be seen with among people who cared about that sort of thing. He was also good-looking in a just-got-out-of-bed way, and Daniel suspected there was more than a culinary motive behind Gloria's sudden interest in cooking. "How long?"

"Three glorious months in Paris, darling. Oh, and you'll need to make arrangements for Jasmine over the summer—actually, immediately. The school called while I was at the spa earlier." She sighed dramatically. "I'm afraid she's been suspended for the remainder of the term."

"Suspended?"

"Some snafu I'm sure you can clear up with a phone call. Just mention Daddy's name every other sentence. That should help."

"I'm a little busy here, Gloria. Why don't you call the school? Meanwhile I'll talk to Jasmine."

"I already spoke with her. She's distraught, poor thing. I wish there were some way I could get up there. She's in desperate need of comfort, but my plane leaves JFK at six. You know what traffic's going to be like, and I haven't even begun to pack."

Daniel's lips tightened to hold back an explosion of words that began somewhere around, How about for once in your life thinking of someone other than yourself? And ended with the words he knew were inevitable. "I'll take care of it."

"Oh, Danny, you're such a good father. I'll phone from Paris. Au revoir, darling." The line went dead.

Daniel's head was spinning, as was often the case following a conversation with his ex. He sucked in deep breaths of what passed for fresh air in the city as he sorted through this particular crisis. Their sixteen-year-old daughter had been suspended from the upstate boarding school they had signed her up for when she was still in the womb. Gloria was off to Paris for the foreseeable future.

And Daniel—as usual—was left to do damage control for them both.

He punched in a number.

"Hi, Daddy, I was just thinking about you." His daughter's voice was too bright, too cheerful and too over-the-top. The fact that she answered immediately told him she'd been expecting his call.

"Your mother called."

Silence.

Daniel forced himself to remain calm. "What happened?"

"It's the headmaster, Daddy. He hates me. He's had it in for me since I arrived. He—"

"What happened?"

"You'll just take their side like you always do," Jazz accused, her tone slipping effortlessly from sweet to the more familiar sullen. "At least M*ama*…" She accented the last syllable, as if speaking French. It was the only parental name Gloria would acknowledge.

"Jasmine, your mother is not available. I'm offering to hear your side of things."

"Why can't you just assume that I'm the wronged party here? Mama would be on the phone—"

"Well, M*ama* is off to cooking school in Paris for three months, so you're stuck with me." His tone hardened. "Since you aren't ready to discuss this rationally, I'll leave now. Get yourself packed just in case I can't work things out—again."

"Just call the airline, Dad. You don't have to come." She sounded bored and a little exasperated that he was making such a big deal of this.

"I am coming there, Jasmine, understood?"

A pause, followed by an uncertain "Whatever."

The next call Daniel made was to Greg, who assured him he could handle everything and would have a car waiting at the side entrance within fifteen minutes. Daniel abandoned the idea of a quiet lunch on the terrace in favor of chomping on an apple as he closed the doors to the terrace and took the elevator back down to the lobby.

On the drive north, Daniel contacted the headmaster and got the gist of what had happened. Jazz had purchased a copy of a midterm exam for a class she'd barely attended all semester. When she had aced the exam, her instructor had become suspicious and things had evolved from there.

"I'm sure you understand that this cannot be overlooked, Mr. Armstrong, even for a student like Jasmine."

Interpretation? Even if Jasmine's grandfather has just contributed a new state-of-the-art student center that bears his name.

"I wouldn't expect the school to overlook it," Daniel replied. "I would question the school's motives if you didn't see this matter as a serious breach of ethics."

Silence, then a tight-lipped "I see." Clearly the headmaster had prepared himself for a battle. "We'd be willing to reinstate Jasmine for the fall term. Of course, she'll be held back a term. We just feel that perhaps she needs to have some consequence for her poor choices in this matter."

"Let's just take things one day at a time," Daniel said. "I'm leaving now and should be there by noon, at the latest."

"I'll have my assistant meet you in Jasmine's dormitory, and the three of you can go over everything together at that time."

Got it, Daniel thought. The mention of the assistant was a reminder that the headmaster functioned in the same world of proper channels as his wealthy benefactors. Fortunately, ten years of living in Gloria's world had taught him a thing or two about the hierarchy of power plays. The headmaster himself would have dealt directly with Gloria or her father. For the ex-husband, an assistant would do.

"Fine," Daniel muttered as he abruptly hung up the phone. "We'll play by your rules—for now."

Jo Cooper hitched one strap of her bibbed overalls back onto her shoulder and headed from the small guest cottage up to the gray-shingled farmhouse. On her way she paused to look out toward the large freshwater pond that sparkled in the morning sun like its name, Star Pond. She closed her eyes and allowed the gentle winds to play over her face, sniffing the clear air as the May sun warmed her cheeks.

Spring was her favorite season—so alive with possibilities. These days the possibility that held the most excitement for Jo was the new business she'd started with one of her six brothers. They had brought the concept of temp workers from the corporate office to the farm—recognizing that a number of aging farmers could use seasonal help getting crops planted, watching over them through the growing season and bringing them to harvest.

Ella Armstrong, a spry, elderly Nantucket widow, had hired them to manage her ten acres of cranberry beds. And although Jo had been a little taken aback when she learned the farm was located on Nantucket Island—not in Maine where her business was based—something in Ella's manner had struck a chord with her. Her brother Hank assured her he could manage the work they'd taken on in Maine. If necessary, he'd draft other family members to pitch in.

"Go," he'd told her. "I think you need this. I think this woman reminds you of Mom."

Their mother had died in a freak accident the year before. Jo had immediately taken over the dual roles of housekeeper and confidant that her mother had performed for a house filled with men.

"You've never had a chance to really mourn. I mean,

you lost her, too, but you've been so busy taking care of Dad and the rest of us… Just do it, okay?"

Jo had arrived on Nantucket in late March, spent that first night in Ella's kitchen going over plans for the season and moved into the guest cottage the following morning. "You'll be wanting your privacy," Ella had told her when Jo had protested that one of the small bedrooms upstairs in the farmhouse was all she needed. "And frankly, I like my privacy as well."

The woman pulled no punches, and in that she reminded Jo a lot of her own mother.

"Joanna Alissa Cooper," her mother had announced one evening when Jo was ten. She had come running home in tears to complain about some prank her brothers had pulled on her. "You are the lone girl in a family of six brothers and you have a choice to make. Either you find the gumption to stand up for yourself, or let them have the upper hand by default. This is not my problem. Do I make myself clear?"

So Jo had watched and learned, and every time she refused to surrender to the teasing and practical jokes her brothers dished out, she saw her mother's proud smile. When Jo started giving as good as she got, the tables were turned and it was her brothers who complained to their mother. But Mom just shrugged, murmured, "Poor babies," and then winked at Jo.

Being with Ella Armstrong had already begun to pay off. For the first time since her mom's accident, she found herself focusing on the way her mom had lived instead of the way she had died.

"Ella," she called as she bounded up the back-porch steps and rapped on the door. As was their routine, Jo was there to share breakfast with Ella. Ella insisted on starting the day with a reading from a daily devotional and silent prayer. Jo maintained a polite silence during both rituals. Her faith, once unshakable, had suffered following her mother's death. She rapped a second time and then paused before opening the back door. Something wasn't right. Every morning since her arrival, Jo had been greeted by the tantalizing smells of bacon frying, cinnamon rolls or blueberry muffins baking and coffee brewing.

She wrenched open the door, stood a split second taking in the pristine kitchen, undisturbed from the night before, and headed at a run for the stairs.

"Ella!"

Ella Armstrong lay on her side on the floor next to her bed. "Good morning, dear. I fell," she said weakly when Jo burst into the room.

"Stay where you are. I'm calling for help." Jo urgently pulled out her cell phone.

"Bother," Ella muttered as Jo gave the dispatcher information while grabbing a pillow and quilt from the bed and making Ella as comfortable as possible on the floor.

"I just have to go unhook the front-door latch," Jo said. "Don't move."

Her work boots thudded on the wooden stairway as she rushed downstairs. Her heart pounded in her ears as she clicked the latch and then immediately sped back upstairs. She was breathing harder on the return and stood for a moment in the doorway, uncertain of what to do next.

"Sit down," Ella instructed weakly. "They'll be here. Probably all excited to get a call. Now if, as I suspect, I've gone and fractured something, I do *not* want you to play nursemaid. Are we clear about that?"

"Yes, ma'am."

Within minutes the ambulance came screaming up the long, winding drive. While the paramedics examined Ella and transferred her to a gurney, Jo called her crew and gave them instructions for the day. "I'm going to the hospital with Mrs. Armstrong," she said into the phone.

"No," Ella protested.

"Yes, I am," Jo said quietly to the older woman, grasping her hand. "So stop arguing."

"Oh, all right. Get my purse. You'll need my Medicare card and such. No bigger than a minute," she added, addressing one of the paramedics, "but bossy as they come."

Jazz slumped in the front passenger seat while Daniel and the headmaster's assistant loaded her things into the trunk.

The assistant had been waiting with Jazz and all her belongings in the lobby of the dorm. As soon as Daniel had arrived, the assistant had come out to meet him, pulling two of Jazz's larger bags. Jazz had followed, carrying only her purse. In the lobby beyond the automatic glass doors, Daniel could see several additional pieces of luggage and two cardboard moving boxes.

Daniel stepped out of the car.

"Mr. Armstrong? Evan Dickson." The young man wore a navy blue blazer embroidered with the school's crest over the left pocket. He set down the suitcases and extended his hand. It was evident by the way he failed to meet Daniel's eyes directly that he was nervous. He offered Daniel a clipboard full of papers that he'd tucked under one arm in order to manage the suitcases. "You'll need to sign these, sir. While you do that, I'll just get everything loaded into—"

Daniel smiled and placed his hands in his pockets, leaving the clipboard dangling between them. "Is the headmaster in his office?" Daniel didn't wait for a response but took Jazz by the elbow, ready to cross the commons to the administration building. To his surprise, Evan Dickson made a blocking move and once again thrust the clipboard at him.

"The headmaster has a lunch meeting. He's asked me to handle this matter."

Daniel bristled inwardly but forced a smile. "Then I'll wait until he is available."

Evan's eyes widened with panic. It was clear that he had been sent on a mission and that he had not reckoned with Daniel being on a mission of his own—to do whatever it took to keep Jazz in school until the end of the term.

"I'm sure we can work all of this out," he assured Evan and made another move toward the commons.

Once again Evan blocked his way.

"Look, Evan, I can see that you have a job to do, but surely you can appreciate my need to speak directly with the headmaster. My daughter has made a serious mistake and I completely agree that she needs to rectify that, but—"

Behind him he heard Jazz's bored sigh, a carbon copy of her mother's. "Give it up, Dad. You know the deal—three strikes and you're out." She pushed herself away from the front fender and relieved Evan of the clipboard. She shuffled through a few pages and read aloud. "Overnight curfew violation equals strike one."

"Overnight?" Daniel's mind reeled with the very idea of his daughter out on her own overnight.

Jazz shrugged. "A few of us decided to go into the city for some shopping—we missed the last train. No biggie."

"And spent the night where?" Daniel demanded.

"Walking around Times Square with about eight gazillion tourists." Jazz actually shuddered at the memory. "It was horrid, so we ended up at Mom's penthouse sometime around two and took the noon train back here."

"And no one thought to let her parents know she was

missing?" Daniel focused his attention on Evan and forced the words through gritted teeth.

"Lighten up. They called Mom and she straightened everything out."

"And strike two?" Daniel was almost afraid to hear this one.

Jazz passed the clipboard back to Evan. "Does it really matter? Let's just go, okay?"

Although he was seriously tempted to grab his daughter by her bony shoulders and shake her until her teeth rattled, as his own mother had often threatened when he pulled stunts like this, Daniel forced himself to remain calm. He held out his hand for the clipboard.

"There are several places to sign," Evan instructed anxiously as he offered Daniel an expensive fountain pen. "All highlighted."

Daniel signed the spaces on the fluttering white pages attached to the clipboard, scrawling his name with such vehemence that in a couple of places the point of the pen punctured the paper. He noticed that one of the things he was promising with his signature was not to hold the school liable or responsible in any way for the issues that had resulted in this suspension. He re-capped the fountain pen before handing it and the clipboard back to a clearly relieved Evan.

"That it?"

"Yes, sir. Thank you, sir." The assistant invited a second handshake and, in spite of the ludicrousness of the gesture, Daniel accepted it. "If you'll just pop the trunk, sir," he added with a glance back at the pile of bags and boxes still stacked in the lobby.

"Jazz, get your stuff," Daniel ordered, and for once Jazz did not argue.

By the time Daniel and the assistant had fit everything

into the trunk and backseat, and Daniel had taken his place behind the wheel, Jazz was on her cell phone. Daniel took it from her, flipped it closed and dropped it in his left breast pocket. "Buckle up," he said quietly.

Jazz rolled her eyes, sighed dramatically and savagely ripped the seat belt across her, snapping it into place. Then she placed her feet on the seat, wrapped her arms around her knees and glared out the window.

A thousand questions ran through Daniel's mind, most of them directed not at Jazz but at himself—and Gloria. Where had they gone wrong? When had the darling little girl who had once enchanted everyone around her turned from that loving, giving, curious child into this?

Daniel took a long, steadying breath as he navigated the long, tree-lined drive that led to the main road. "Look, Jazz, we need to work this thing out. Your mother's off to Paris, and I have the hotel to run and—"

"Yeah, it's all about you and Mom. I get it." She pulled farther into the cocoon she'd created by hugging her knees and gazing out the window.

"That's not what I meant," Daniel replied tersely. "Why is it that everything I say to you gets misinterpreted? I am simply making the point that we have some—"

"Everybody does it, buys answers," Jazz scoffed as if he'd asked about the pirated exam.

"No, everybody doesn't." He was about to expound on the old "and if everybody decided to jump off the Brooklyn Bridge" concept when his phone vibrated.

"Daniel?" It was Greg. Daniel left it on speaker mode.

"What's up?" Automatically Daniel began thinking about the hotel, the groups scheduled to arrive, the special arrangements to be overseen.

"The hospital called," Greg said. "Nantucket. It's your mom."

"Grandma?" Jazz whispered, and for the first time released her grip on her knees and turned her attention to her father.

"They wouldn't tell me much. She fell and they've got her there. I have the number."

Jazz pulled open the glove compartment and found a pen and paper.

"Go," Daniel said.

Greg dictated the number and Jazz wrote it down.

"Got it. Thanks."

As soon as the call ended, Jazz dialed the number for the hospital. It was rare moments like this when Daniel felt the faintest spark of hope that just maybe the loving, caring kid she'd once been was still there, somewhere underneath that tough veneer of boredom and entitlement.

The phone at the other end rang three times. "Nantucket Cottage Hospital."

It took less than a minute for the receptionist to get him through to intensive care, but by the time she did Daniel's hands were gripping the steering wheel so tightly that his knuckles had gone white. Jazz placed her hand on his and he relaxed slightly.

The news was not as bad as he had feared. His seventy-four-year-old mother had fallen and fractured her hip. She had also hit her head. She was in intensive care for observation overnight. If everything went well, she would move to a regular room the following day. The doctors were assessing the need for a hip replacement. At the very least she would need intensive rehabilitation and physical therapy.

"Please tell my mother that I'll be there tonight."

"I'll need my phone," Jazz said as soon as he hung up. "I want to stay in touch with you about Grandma."

"We're both going to Nantucket, Jazz. We'll stop at the hotel so I can pack and then head for the airport."

"But I can stay at Mom's—really. The rest of my stuff is there."

"Let's get this settled right now, Jazz. While your mother is away, you'll be staying with me and you'll make do with the stuff back there." He jerked his head toward the backseat and trunk of the car.

Any progress Daniel might have thought they'd made when the call had come about his mother was erased in an instant as Jazz's features settled back into the hardened mask of the long-suffering.

Chapter Two

Jo was on her way back to the intensive care waiting room after grabbing a salad for her supper when she spotted the man and the teenager. He was dressed in an obviously expensive charcoal business suit, jacket unbuttoned, scarlet silk tie pulled loose, top button of his shirt collar open. He had a full head of wavy hair, the color of wet sand. He was tall and stood before the waiting room receptionist with legs spread as if to maintain his balance on a ship as the deck beneath his feet roiled and dipped. In spite of that, he looked worn down, broad shoulders sagging, handsome face lined with worry.

The teen cleared her throat, drawing Jo's attention. They stared, each eyeing the other as if she were a visitor from outer space. The girl wore far too much makeup and clothes that exposed too much skin. A tiny leather jacket that Jo was sure held no more warmth than the girl's expression had been casually abandoned on the nearest chair.

"Excuse me," Jo said, moving past the girl and addressing the man. When he turned, she watched as his astonishing deep blue eyes swept over her and in the same instant labeled her. She saw him take in the faded overalls, the plaid flannel shirt frayed at the cuffs and collar, the scuffed work boots, all before he met her gaze. She straightened to her full height and still came only to the tip of his chin, shadowed now with the start of a sandy beard.

"Oh, Jo," the receptionist interjected. "This is Mrs. Armstrong's son, Daniel. He's just arrived. Jo found your mother," she hastened to explain. "She was the one who called the paramedics," she added in a tone that indicated she thought Daniel should be on his knees in gratitude.

Instead he frowned. "How did she fall?"

"I don't know. She was on the floor when I found her."

He abruptly turned back to the receptionist. "I'd like to see her."

"Of course." The receptionist made a call and then indicated the automated double doors behind her.

"Thank you," Daniel muttered. "Jazz, come on."

Jo watched as the teen unfurled herself from the chair, grabbed the leather jacket and walked past Jo and the receptionist with the long, hips-forward stride and expressionless face of a fashion model.

"I guess I'll go," Jo said. "I'll be at this number if anyone asks." She jotted down her cell number on a notepad and handed it to the receptionist. Not that she expected anyone to call. After all, she was just the temp farmer that Ella had hired to manage her cranberry bog. Ella's family was here now—the son she talked about with equal amounts of pride at his success and exasperation at his failure to find a "good woman" and the granddaughter she worried about constantly.

To Daniel's relief, one of the doctors assigned to his mother's case was still in the hospital and apprised him of Ella's condition and prognosis.

"Assuming she has no further trauma overnight, we can move her out of ICU tomorrow and move forward on repairing that hip," reported the young man who didn't look old enough to be out of college, much less out of medical school.

"She's been complaining about that hip for years—claims she can tell the weather by it." Daniel's voice cracked.

The doctor cleared his throat. "Well, I hate to take away her barometer, but she's a good candidate for hip replacement. She's in excellent condition for a woman of her age. In fact, when they brought her in, we had to check the age twice."

"Prognosis?"

"I expect she'll come through the surgery with flying colors. After that there'll be a lengthy period of therapy and rehabilitation."

"I'll start checking out facilities in New York."

"Oh, that's not necessary. She'll spend some time in the rehab unit here to get the basics down, and then the rest can be handled through home care services. Your mother will need the family's support, of course."

"You mean send her home? To Star Pond?" Daniel shook his head and saw Jazz's eyes widen in alarm. "I'm afraid that's impossible. I have a business to run and—" His mind raced with the image of the three of them all together in that hotel suite.

"Look, take some time to think this through. But consider this—research has shown that folks at your mom's stage of life do better if there's not too much disruption to the routine they've settled into. Especially following some traumatic event such as this one." He shrugged. "Just give it some thought. And given her clarity of mind, Mrs. Armstrong needs to be part of any decision you make."

"She's in no shape to—"

The doctor stood up and so did Daniel. "It's her life," the doctor said, offering a handshake before he turned to go.

Daniel left Jazz in the waiting room while he went back to see his mother. This time she was awake, and she perked up when she saw him. "Have to do what I can to get you over here for a visit," she said with a smile.

"This might have been a little extreme. A phone call would have sufficed." He held her hand.

"I thought I heard Jasmine earlier."

"She's here."

"You took her out of school to come here?"

"She's been suspended for the remainder of the term." The one thing Daniel had always been with both his parents was completely honest. Neither of them had ever been able to tolerate beating about the bush, as they called it, to protect someone.

Ella rolled her eyes and sighed, then she brightened. "She could spend the summer with me on the farm. Do her good. She can help Jo with the berries."

"Mom, who is this Jo?"

"I told you about her. She's the temp I hired to manage this year's crop. Joanna Cooper. She's from Maine."

"Temp? As in a kind of personal assistant?" Daniel thought back to the petite woman in overalls and boots that he'd seen in the waiting room.

"Oh, do come into the twenty-first century, Daniel. Temp as in farmer for hire. You city business types aren't the only ones who can benefit from the help of short-term workers." She paused. "Her family's in the cranberry business in Maine. She and one of her brothers got this idea to start this business. I heard about it from Cyrus Banks—he's become a regular Internet fanatic. I'm so glad I hired her—she's been amazing."

"She's barely taller than Jazz and can't weigh more than a hundred pounds. How old is she, anyway? And how can she—"

Ella's eyes twinkled. "Why, Danny, you finally really looked at a woman worthy of your notice. For you, that's major progress. How is Gloria these days?" But suddenly Ella grimaced with pain and Daniel reached for the call bell. "Stop that," his mother ordered, swatting weakly at his hand. "They'll be here directly to give me the next dose of this stuff that puts me in la-la land. Now, you listen to me while I can still think clearly. I want you and Jazz to go to the farm and—"

"We'll get a room at the White Elephant," Daniel interrupted.

"Stop throwing your money away like you're still a Barrington," she snapped. "Go to the farm. You'll have to stay in the house. I gave Jo the cottage."

"You what?"

"Part of her salary. Place is just sitting there and she needs a place to stay and there you have it."

A nurse moved around the bed to change the drip bag connected to Ella's left arm. "Mrs. Armstrong," she announced in a voice loud enough to be heard in the next room.

"Don't shout, dear. I'm old but my hearing is fine."

"Well, you need your rest," the nurse replied in a softer tone as she glanced meaningfully at Daniel. "You can see your family tomorrow."

Daniel leaned down and kissed his mother's forehead. "Sleep well," he whispered, but saw that she was already half-asleep.

On the drive to the farm, Jazz curled into a ball of discontent and scowled at him. The minute he'd informed her that they would not be staying at the inn or enjoying a long-overdue dinner at one of the island's many fine restaurants, she had punished him with her silence.

"Think of it as doing something for your grandmother," he said. As he parked the rental car next to the house, he took note of the single lamp glowing from the cottage's front room and the rusty red truck parked in front.

"I don't get it," Jazz groused. "I mean, is there even anything to eat in this place?"

Daniel slammed the car door—it had already been quite a day. If Gloria jetting off to Paris and leaving him to deal with Jazz's suspension wasn't bad enough, now he had to make a major decision about his mother's care. And on top of all that, he'd left the hotel lobby filled with guests complaining about the slow check-in process in an establishment that hoped to build its reputation on service.

Exactly how am I supposed to be in three places at the same time? he wondered.

He gazed up at the night sky, hoping the fresh sea air and clear, starlit night would calm him. Instead he caught sight of a jet heading east over the Atlantic. *Bon voyage, Gloria,* he thought bitterly, although her plane was no doubt already well on its way across the Atlantic. *You go play chef. Don't worry about a thing. I've got it all under control—as usual.*

"Dad?" He realized that Jazz had been yammering on about the catastrophic turn of events that had her leaving school, banished to a clapboard farmhouse in a provincial town that was bereft of all the creature comforts of her world.

He tossed her the extra set of house keys that were always to be found under a huge conch shell by the back steps. "Why don't you get settled? I just have to check on something." He headed across the yard.

Jo had just reached to close the blinds in the living room when she heard the knock. She glanced at the clock. After eleven. She sighed.

Of course she'd heard the car come up the road, seen

the headlights fan over the cottage, heard the muffled voices of Ella's son and granddaughter—his tired and world-weary; hers borderline whining. "But Dad…" had echoed across the yard, followed by the slam of a car door.

A second knock—more insistent than the first. Jo opened the door. He was leaning against the door frame, one hand thrust into his pants pocket, the other raised to knock a third time. He looked both exhausted and at the same time like some cover hero from one of those romance novels Ella was so fond of reading.

Jo watched him take in the pink bunny slippers peeking out from the hem of her jeans. "How's Ella?" she asked.

"Can I come in for a minute?" he said at the same moment.

Jo swung the door wide and stood aside as he stepped into the small, over-furnished room and looked around. It was as if he'd stepped into a place that was familiar and yet not what he expected. From the kitchen the whistle of a teakettle punctuated the silence. "Have a seat. I was just about to have a little chamomile tea," she said, and escaped to the kitchen.

She took her time pouring milk into a small pitcher, slicing a lemon, searching the cabinets for mugs that matched. As Ella had laughingly told her when she'd moved in, "*Guest cottage* is a bit of a misnomer. Through the years we've used it for any number of purposes— mostly a place to put furniture and other junk we no longer use at the main house but truly believe might come in handy someday."

She heard Ella's son clear his throat. "Almost ready," she called as she pulled open a drawer and grabbed teaspoons, then thought of the honey. Ella liked honey in her tea and perhaps so did her son. "Sorry," she said as she set the tray on the coffee table, then immediately wondered why she should apologize.

He nodded acceptance of the apology and reached for the teapot. Clear, hot water trickled out. "Needs to steep," he said, setting the pot back down. He removed the lid and was prepared to pour the water from his mug back when they both noticed the problem.

"I forgot to add the tea bags," Jo muttered. "Sorry."

"I'll get them," he said, rising before she could. "Do you still keep them in the canister on the counter?"

Jo nodded.

After he returned and dunked three bags into the steaming water several times, Jo poured for both of them. He fingered the jar of honey.

"Cyrus Banks," he murmured, reading the handwritten label. "Is he still keeping bees?"

"Yes. I've arranged for him to bring his hives over as soon as the vines start to flower. We got off to a late start this season, but I expect to have the hives in place sometime in the next few weeks." Jo had pulled herself together enough to realize that Ella's son had probably come to talk business. After all, he would be in charge. At least until Ella could come home—and maybe even then.

"I'd like to speak with you about my mother," he said. He was looking directly at her over the rim of his mug and she realized that he was taking the measure of her as a possible ally.

"Go on," she said quietly.

"She's no spring chicken. She lives here alone. Her bedroom and bath are on the second floor. I think you can see where this is going?"

"Not really, but I would hazard a guess that you are concerned about her continuing to live here on the farm?"

"On the farm—on this island." He set down his mug and ran a hand through his hair. "She's going to need care, Ms. Cooper, a *lot* of care."

"It's Jo, and it's too soon to assess just what her long-term needs might be."

He stood up and Jo saw the change in position for the unconscious power play that it was. "She's got a fractured hip."

"Yes, and as I understand it, the success rate for hip replacement is quite impressive. Ella is in good health and she's—"

He waved a dismissive hand at her and changed the subject. "That's not the point. The point is that eventually—and sooner rather than later—there will have to be changes. The question I want to pose to you is whether or not it makes any sense at all to invest in bringing in a cranberry crop that, for at least the last decade, has been more work than it's worth."

Jo did not like where this conversation was headed. "As opposed to?"

"As opposed to preparing the land—and the house and outbuildings—for sale."

"Are you firing me, Mr. Armstrong?"

"I'm not even sure what it is you do," he said with an exasperated frown. "No, I'm not asking you to leave, but I thought perhaps… You see, Mom's going to need help in the house until I can put together a plan—a kind of caregiver and—" He stopped at the look of pure astonishment Jo gave him. "I mean, whatever Mom is paying you I would double it. She's going to have to have help until I can make other arrangements.

"What kind of help?" Jo asked hesitantly.

"Cooking, cleaning, getting dressed and bathed," he replied.

"I think you may have misinterpreted my position here, Mr. Armstrong. What I do is manage farms for people like your mother who need someone to oversee the planting, raising and harvesting of crops—primarily cranberries. My family has been in the business of raising cranberries in Maine for five generations." She gave him a level gaze. "My youngest brother and I started this business last fall. He's handling our clients back on the mainland and I came here."

Daniel seemed about to interrupt but Jo was on a roll. "I have a master's degree in agricultural science and, before going out on my own, I worked for the nation's premiere cranberry processing company as a manager of quality control. Your mother and I have a contract for my services." She crossed her arms. "I do not work for you. Neither am I qualified to cook, clean or be a nursemaid. As I've just demonstrated, I have trouble making a pot of tea. In short, Mr. Armstrong, I do not do windows."

She stood up and walked to the front door. "Now, if you'll excuse me—it's been a long day and tomorrow promises more of the same."

He followed her to the door and started down the path, then turned back. "Why did you leave the corporate job? The money must have been better than this—plus benefits?"

"The work was inside," she answered without hesitation.

His eyes narrowed in confusion. "And?"

"I like being outside." She shut the door, leaving him standing on the cobblestone stoop. After a long moment she heard the crunch of his city loafers on the clamshell fragments of the path.

Chapter Three

The following morning Daniel awoke to the gray fog and mist that was one source—along with the perennially gray shingled structures—of the island's nickname, Little Gray Lady of the Sea. On his way to the lone bathroom at the end of the upstairs hall, he tapped on the closed door of Jazz's room. "Start getting ready," he said. "We need to get to the hospital."

A muffled groan told him he'd been heard. He showered and shaved and dressed in his suit pants and the clean shirt he always carried in his computer bag. On his way downstairs, he knocked on Jazz's door again. This time he opened it and left it open. "Rise and shine," he bellowed.

"Dad! Take a chill pill," she protested.

In the kitchen Daniel turned on the coffeemaker and prepared bowls of instant oatmeal he found in his mother's well-stocked pantry. "Jasmine, now!"

"It's freezing," she grumbled ten minutes later when she finally appeared with the quilt from her bed draped over her shoulders. She slouched into a kitchen chair, then took note of the headset Daniel wore as he conducted the dual business of making breakfast in Nantucket and running a hotel in Manhattan. "Do I get my phone back today?"

Daniel held up one finger. "And Greg, call me if there's anything major. I know you've got everything covered, but keep me in the loop. Yeah. Bye." He set a bowl of oatmeal in front of Jazz. "I left your phone and laptop at the hotel when we stopped to get my things. No phone until the end of the school year, and then we'll discuss the matter."

Her mouth formed an O of pure horror. "You're joking."

"Not so much," Daniel replied as he took the chair across from her and dug into his oatmeal, all the while entering notes on his phone's day planner between bites. When she didn't say anything he glanced at her. She sat with folded arms staring daggers at him. "Eat up and then get dressed."

"I'm going back to bed," she announced defiantly.

Daniel considered this. He needed to focus on his mother and finding out from the doctors whether or not she could get the care she needed here on the island. He was prepared to have her transferred to a hospital in Manhattan, just in case. If he didn't have to worry about Jazz while he attended to all that, he could be more efficient. Besides, what trouble could she get into here?

"Sounds like a plan. You go back to bed and I'll be home by lunch." He opened the refrigerator. "We'll need to pick up some stuff. Make a list, okay?"

Her eyes widened with surprise at his capitulation, followed by wariness. "Just how long are we staying?"

"As long as we need—until I can figure out what's best for Grandma." Jazz looked as if she'd just been blindsided, and Daniel actually felt a little sorry for her. "Honey, I know neither of us saw this coming, but Grandma needs us. Okay?"

Her eyes brimmed with tears. "Is Grandma going to be okay or is she going to be—you know—like, crippled or something?"

Daniel could see that this question only touched the surface of what went unasked. The truth was that many of the same questions were racing through his head. He hugged her hard, then let her go. "I'll have more information on that by lunchtime, okay?"

Jazz nodded and headed for the stairs. For a moment Daniel envied her youth and wished he could turn back the clock to the days when he, too, had no cares because he knew his parents would handle everything. Now he was the parent. Now his father was gone, and his mother, looking more frail than he'd ever thought possible, needed him.

As he rinsed out the dishes, he saw Jo leaning out the driver's side of her battered pickup and talking to a man in a bigger truck. She was dressed in bright yellow rain gear, the hood pulled up and concealing everything but the lower half of her face. Through the glass of the kitchen window he heard her laugh—a laugh that he found amazingly feminine and attractive. For a woman who carried herself like a tomboy, the sound made him look twice to be certain of its source.

By the time he arrived at the hospital, Ella had already been moved out of intensive care.

"The bone is still properly aligned," the doctor explained. "So we could perform a procedure called internal fixation."

"Plain talk, Doc," Ella said.

"We put in metal screws to hold the bone in place while the fracture heals."

"But?" She had always been an expert at reading between the lines.

The doctor smiled. "But if you were my mother I'd suggest a total hip replacement. Given your age—"

"Watch it, sonny," Ella teased.

"You've experienced some arthritis in that hip before. I understand you can actually predict the weather?"

"Only the occasional nor'easter," Ella admitted. "So, when can you do this thing?"

"Mom, let's talk about this," Daniel interjected.

"We just did. The doctor's right. Cyrus Banks had that surgery three years ago and you should see him. He's better than ever—always bragging about having a new spring in his step. Sounds to me like the metal screws would end up being a temporary fix."

"We could do the surgery late tomorrow afternoon."

"Then what?" she demanded.

"Well, you won't exactly hop off the operating table. You'll probably need to be here at least through the weekend so we can get you started on some rehab therapy. After that we can send you home with home care services." He turned his attention to Daniel. "You can check with Social Services. They'll send someone out to the house to go over modifications you might need to make there."

Daniel was speechless. Did this guy not get it? His mother lived alone—on a farm—five miles from town. Her only son had a demanding job in Manhattan. Exactly how was this supposed to work?

"Well, you get some rest now," the doctor told Ella, squeezing her hand as he nodded to Daniel and left the room. They could hear him greet the patient across the hall, much the same as he had greeted Ella ten minutes earlier.

"Mom, we have to discuss this," Daniel said.

Ella's smile changed instantly to a scowl, one that reminded Daniel of his daughter. "There is nothing to discuss, Daniel. You heard the doctor. This is the way to go—the fastest way to get me up and around again so we can all get back to our normal lives."

Exactly what was normal anymore? Daniel wondered.

In just twenty-four hours enough had changed that he doubted he'd ever see normal again.

"Let's get a second opinion, at least. I've got everything set to have you transferred to Cedars and—"

"And suppose they say the same thing?"

"Then you'll have the surgery. They have some of the best surgeons in the country."

"Oh, come off your high horse. There is nothing miraculous about those doctors just because they practice in New York City. That city is a madhouse—fun to visit, but do *not* ask me to have surgery there."

Daniel knew better than to pursue the matter further, at least for the time being. "I brought you the paper," he said, handing Ella the weekly *Nantucket Telegraph Inquirer.*

"Give me the headlines," Ella said, relaxing onto the pillows and closing her eyes. In five minutes she was sound asleep.

"Mr. Armstrong?" A middle-aged woman stood at the door. "I'm Barbara Chase, from Social Services?"

Daniel stood and extended his hand. "Let's talk outside," he said.

Finally, he thought, someone who might actually understand that Ella returning to that farmhouse was impossible.

"Hey! Get out of there," Jo shouted when one of the two men she'd hired to set up the sprinkler system pointed out the girl walking through the newly planted cranberry bed. Jo recognized her from the night before and saw that once again her choice of clothing was totally inappropriate for both the weather and the setting. "Out!" she yelled, and started across one of the dikes toward where the girl had sunk ankle deep into the rain-soaked sand, flailing as she tried to pull herself free and remain upright.

"Climb up right here," Jo ordered when she got close enough.

"I'm stuck." The girl reeked of attitude.

"Well, get yourself unstuck and get out of there." Jo looked around and saw a length of the sprinkler pipe the crew had been putting together. "Here, grab on." Jo lay down on her stomach and stretched the pipe toward the girl, who looked at it as if it were a cobra.

"It's all yucky," she shouted.

"That's called rust—it washes off. Now, grab on or stay there until your dad gets back. At least if you're stuck you can't trample any more innocent plants."

The girl glanced around. Her long hair—the same color as her father's—was wet and plastered against her face and the shoulders of her leather jacket. One of those oversize shawls that were big sellers in the city was looped around her throat. Under the short jacket she wore a long, fitted T-shirt that covered her hips. Her jeans were tucked into knee-high boots.

"Can you lose the boots? That might help."

"Do you have any idea what these boots cost? They are designer originals, not some cheap knockoff. Just figure out something else."

"Excuse me? I was sure I heard you demand help just thirty seconds ago." Jo put down the pipe and stood up. If she were still a praying woman, she might be begging God for patience. "I've got work to do. You figure it out, but if you so much as touch any more of those plants…"

"Where are you going? You can't leave me here. It's pouring. I'll catch pneumonia!"

"It's a light drizzle, and perhaps you should have considered that when you got dressed this morning." Jo paused. "Where were you headed, anyway?" A sudden fear gripped her. "It's not your grandmother, is it?" She'd seen Ella's son drive away earlier and taken note of the fact that his daughter was not with him. Maybe something had happened and the girl—upset and irrational—had tried to get to the hospital.

"Just please get me out of here," the girl begged, her features contrite, and Jo began to actually feel genuine sympathy for the kid.

She lay back down on the ground and extended the pipe. The girl wrapped her scarf around it before taking hold. Jo tugged and the girl fell forward. She came up spitting sand and Jo saw the men working across the way turn away, their hands covering their laughter. Even so, their muffled chuckles drifted across the open berry beds. The girl glared up at them and then at Jo.

"Look, your feet popped free—expensive boots and all. Now hang on to the pole and walk carefully this way." Once she had her safely on the dike, Jo took off her slicker and handed it to the girl. "Put this on," she instructed, then turned to her crew. "I'm taking her back to the house," she shouted.

One of the men waved.

"This way," Jo said. "That's my truck there."

It took less than five minutes to reach the house, but nevertheless the girl's teeth were chattering and her shoulders shook under the oversize slicker. Jo decided the cottage was closer. "Come on. Let's get you into a warm shower and out of those wet clothes."

For once there was no protest.

"Jasmine, right?" Jo said, making small talk as she turned on the shower and helped the kid undress. "Well, Jasmine, a nice, warm shower and a cup of hot tea—maybe some chicken broth. Did you have lunch yet?"

"I can undress myself," Jasmine protested.

"Fine. Leave everything on the floor." She handed Jasmine her terry-cloth robe.

Jasmine held it with two fingers as if it were diseased.

"Take it or go naked," Jo muttered as she exited the bathroom and closed the door. She needed this?

Daniel was at his wit's end. His mother refused to listen to reason and now his daughter was nowhere to be found. He'd been through the house calling her name, checking her room, taking note of the absence of her jacket and scarf. At the same time he'd been momentarily relieved that the rest of her stuff was still spilled across the dresser and unmade bed in the small bedroom. Downstairs nothing had changed since breakfast—dishes as he'd left them— but the phone was off the hook, which explained why he'd gotten a busy signal every time he'd tried calling.

He saw the farmer's red truck by the cottage. Maybe Jo had noticed something. He grabbed one of several rain slickers his parents had kept by the back door since he could remember and started across the yard. He was just about to knock when he heard his daughter's all-too-familiar whine of protest.

"You can't be serious, lady."

Daniel tried the door, found it unlocked and walked in. "What's going on?" he asked as he took in the unlikely scene before him.

Jazz was hunched in a corner of the sofa, wrapped in a wine-colored terry robe. There was a fire in the fireplace and over the screen hung a pair of jeans next to a flimsy, long-sleeved knit top that he recognized as belonging to Jazz.

Jo Cooper was calmly slurping down the last of what he assumed was a bowl of soup. "Completely serious," she was saying as Daniel stepped inside.

"Dad! Do something," Jazz demanded, while Jo barely acknowledged his presence.

"Is there a problem here?" he asked, directing the question to Jo.

"Your daughter apparently got her GPS system out of whack. Seems she was on her way to the airport—a five-mile hike in the opposite direction from where she was headed, I might add. She walked into the middle of the hybrid bed I just planted, uprooting several plants in the process. She got stuck in the wet sand, so I pulled her out and brought her here to dry out." She delivered this information in the same no-nonsense manner with which she had enumerated her résumé the evening before. Then she brushed past him on her way to the kitchen. "Want some soup?" she asked.

"And," Jazz shouted after her, "now Farmer Brown here demands that I show up tomorrow to repair the damage to her precious plants. She actually expects me to work in the fields like some migrant field hand or something."

"The correct term is *bog,* and what do you have against migrant workers?" Jo called from the kitchen.

Daniel frowned and Jazz clearly took that as a signal that he was wavering, so she pressed her case. "I offered to pay for the damage, Dad—out of my own pocket. As soon as I can get to an ATM. I mean, I at least said I was sorry. Unlike *somebody,* who in rescuing me probably destroyed an expensive leather jacket, not to mention my new boots." This last was directed toward the kitchen before Jazz turned back to her father. "I'd say we're even, wouldn't you?"

Before Daniel could reply Jo was back. She handed him a bowl of soup and turned to Jazz. "No, we are not even. The damage to your clothing was your doing—you chose to enter that cranberry bed. As Ella's granddaughter, I assume you are a young woman who takes responsibility for the choices she makes."

"I'm sixteen," Jazz protested.

"Funny, I thought you were older—the way you dress, I mean. But now that you mention it, I can see I was wrong. Someone older would be mature enough to accept responsibility."

"Okay, okay," Daniel said when Jazz looked as if she might actually propel herself off the sofa and attack the farmer. "Let's all settle down. Jazz, what were you doing out in this weather? Where were you going?"

Jazz muttered something.

"I didn't catch that."

"As I mentioned," Jo said, "she tells me she was on her way to the airport."

"Is that true?"

Jazz shrugged and sighed wearily.

"I checked the house before coming here, as well as my voice mail. You were just planning to leave with no explanation?" Feeling suddenly exhausted, Daniel sank down on the opposite end of the sofa.

Jazz buried her face in the crook of her elbow against the back of the sofa and burst into sobs. "I need my phone," she wailed as if her father had denied her the bare essentials of life.

This rendered Daniel speechless. Then he saw Jo hide a smile as she looked at him with raised eyebrows that seemed to ask, What now, Dad?

Daniel deliberately turned his back on that look and forced his concentration on his daughter. "Jasmine, we have got to work out some basic guidelines here. You can't just run off."

The teen's head shot up, her eyes defiant. "Why not? Mom has no problem just up and leaving without so much as a phone call. And you—it takes a major incident to get your attention." She curled herself more tightly into the corner of the sofa.

Daniel felt himself flush—whether with anger or embarrassment that Jo was hearing this he didn't take the time to decide. He turned to Jo. "I wonder if you might give us a moment here. Thank you for what you've done for Jasmine."

Jazz snorted but said nothing.

"Stay as long as you like," Jo replied as she pulled on her rain gear. She glanced over at Jazz. "See you in the morning at seven."

"Dad!"

Daniel heard Jo chuckle as she shut the door on Jazz's cry of protest. She revved her truck and headed back to work.

I could use a little help here, he raged silently at the closed door. But no, instead of minding her own business or offering something in the way of actual assistance and support, little miss farmer was only adding to his problems.

Chapter Four

Jo couldn't help feeling a little sorry for Daniel Armstrong as she assessed the damage the girl had caused. It wasn't that bad. Still, the way Jo saw it the kid would learn nothing from walking away. If Jo made her replant the damaged area, not to mention repairing the sand base she'd managed to disturb, she might think twice the next time. It was unlikely she'd ever come near a cranberry bog again. And of course, the father would need to back up Jo on the kid making restitution.

Unlikely. Daniel Armstrong was one of those men Jo saw often on the island—a man seemingly linked to his work by the invisible wire of a cell phone, BlackBerry or both. Throw into that mix an elderly parent in the hospital and a rebellious teen, and the man had his share of trouble. He would cave to the teen. According to Ella, both her son and his wife had spoiled the child early on and now seemed incapable of taking a stand with her. Jo shook her head and once again counted her blessings that she was single and responsible only for herself.

Not that she didn't want children of her own. One day. Of course, there was the little matter of first finding the appropriate father for those kids, and that just hadn't been in the stars for her so far.

She was well aware that Ella had given some thought to the possibility of introducing Jo to Daniel before now. Ever since Jo had arrived and her bond with Ella had become so close, Ella had mentioned her son on numerous occasions. Of course, Ella's motives had been transparent. And now that the meeting had taken place, Jo was absolutely certain that Daniel probably felt the same way she did about any idea they might hit it off.

So when she returned to the cottage after a long day of fighting the drizzle and chill as they finally completed the setup of the antiquated sprinkler system, she was surprised to find a note propped on the mantel.

Dear Ms. Cooper,
Jasmine and I will be going to the hospital at seven. I'm sure Mom would like to see you as well, if you'd like to ride with us.
Daniel Armstrong

Jo stared at the note for a long time. It was as if this were some code that needed breaking. Why would he offer a ride to the hospital? Why would he not even mention what had happened earlier? Then she smiled as the truth dawned on her. Daniel Armstrong and his daughter were going to try and negotiate the terms of her punishment for damaging the crop. She picked up the phone.

"Mr. Armstrong?" she said when he answered on the first ring. "This is Jo Cooper."

In the background she could hear meat sizzling in a skillet and the whirring of an electric can opener. She looked out the window, across the yard to Ella's kitchen window. He was standing at the sink, the receiver of Ella's outdated wall phone lodged between his shoulder and ear, the cord trailing him as he reached for something on the counter. "You got my note?"

"Yes, and I wanted to thank you for the offer of a ride. Actually, I thought I'd catch a quick shower and then head on over to the hospital now. Ella likes me to update her on the work over supper."

He didn't respond and she could see a plume of smoke curling up from the skillet, activating the smoke alarm. "Okay," he shouted and dropped the phone.

Jo continued to hold her phone and watch the scene across the yard. She saw him touch the skillet and immediately release it. Ouch, she thought with a grimace. Maybe she should go up there. But then she saw him grab a pitcher of water and douse the contents of the skillet, sending up even more smoke and steam as he threw open the window and back door.

Feeling a little too much like a Peeping Tom, Jo clicked off the phone and closed the window blind. "Cooper, you seriously have to think about getting a life," she muttered as she went to take her shower and change.

Daniel couldn't help admitting that Jo Cooper without the baggy overalls and draped in a rain slicker at least two sizes too large got his attention. Now she was wearing fitted black jeans and a bright pink hooded sweater over a paler pink T-shirt. Her skin had the kind of fresh-scrubbed, rosy-cheek quality that—based on his experience with Gloria—he assumed she'd created with foundation and blush. But a closer look under the glare of the hospital room's ceiling lights showed it to be completely natural. She wasn't wearing lipstick and when he leaned past her to give his mother a kiss, it took a moment to realize that her perfume was just plain soap.

"Hello, Daniel," his mother said, then turned her attention to Jazz. "Jasmine, I understand you'll be working with Jo tomorrow. I can't tell you how delighted I am to hear you've taken an interest in the family business."

Daniel saw Jazz glance at Jo and then study her grandmother to see if there was any sarcasm in her praise. Finding none, she searched for a change in subject. "I…uh… Aren't hotels the family business, Grandma?"

"The hotel business is your heritage on your mother's side—and it's your father's profession at the moment. But our family has been on that farm raising the best cranberries on Nantucket for over fifty years. I have to admit that I thought your grandfather was taking an enormous risk when he decided that cranberries would be more profitable than raising sheep."

Jazz grinned. She was obviously relieved to be on the solid ground of this often-told family history. "But that red gold paid a lot of bills, right, Grams?"

Ella smiled. "It'll do you good to learn more about it, and Jo here is just the one to teach you. You stick with her and you'll be surprised what you can learn. You might even get a term paper out of it."

Jo and Jazz exchanged a look and then Jo stood up. "I should be going," she said, speaking directly to Ella. "I'll stop by tomorrow."

Ella touched her hand affectionately.

"See you at seven," Jo said as she passed Jazz on her way to the door. It was not a question and Daniel did not miss the look of pleading his daughter sent his way.

"I'll be right back," he said and followed Jo into the hall. She was already halfway to the bank of elevators. For a woman who barely came to his chin, she had a long stride that covered a lot of territory in a short amount of time. "Ms. Cooper—Jo—could I talk to you?"

She paused and waited for him to catch up. "Ella seems to have rallied well," she said.

"I was wondering…. I mean, I see what you're trying to do with this thing with Jazz, but the truth is she's not much for the outdoors."

Jo continued to meet his gaze with a pleasant half smile on her face, but she said nothing.

"Besides, we came here straight from her school and I don't think she has anything approaching the right wardrobe for working in the bog. I'd like you to reconsider her offer to pay for the damage."

"With your money?"

He ran a hand through his hair, then plunged it into his pocket. He tried a smile. "Look, she's a kid. Any money she has is my money—or her mother's."

He thought the smile had worked. She shifted uncomfortably from one foot to the other and suddenly seemed incapable of meeting his gaze. But just as suddenly she appeared to pull herself together, as her head jerked up and she forced her eyes to meet his. "I assume from what Ella has told me that you've spent your share of time in the bog."

"Yes, but—"

"Then you must be aware that this isn't a simple case of heading to the local garden center and picking up a few plants. These plants are a new hybrid that your mother has been working on for the past few seasons. So your money—or your daughter's—is really of no use here."

"But she understands money—paying for things." At least buying things, he thought.

Jo hoisted her shoulder purse higher on her shoulder. "Look, it's your call. I mean, beyond my setting the terms up front, we both know I have no further power here. If you decide to give in to her…" She left the idea hanging as she pressed the call button for the elevator.

"Why should it matter to you whether I pay you to hire someone to repair the damage or Jazz shows up tomorrow?"

He saw her shoulders straighten and she once again turned to face him. This time, though, she took a step toward him so closely that he could have easily reached out and touched her.

"It's about respect," she said in a low voice. "Respect the hours of work that went into producing those plants in the first place and then preparing and planting that area." She sighed. "Respect for the work. Respect for your mother. Respect for you, if it comes to that. This is your home, your history. Doesn't that matter?"

Daniel stared at her for a long moment. "Do you have children?" he finally managed.

To his surprise she laughed. "Nope. What I have is six brothers. My folks had a thing about respect and you just heard the lecture."

The elevator doors opened and she stepped inside. Then her features softened with empathy. "Look, you've had a pretty rough couple of days. She's your daughter, so whatever you decide is fine," she said. "You've got enough on your plate worrying about Ella. So go ahead and make it easier on yourself and let the kid off the hook."

The doors slid shut and Daniel knew instantly that it was her parting shot that had changed his mind. The respect lecture had been impressive, but now she had challenged his ability to juggle multiple crises. He was the master multitasker when it came to handling catastrophes, and in his entire adult life he had never once asked anyone to make things easier for him. He wasn't about to start with a dark-haired, green-eyed pixie who fancied herself a philosopher as well as a farm manager.

Jo was up at dawn, and experience told her the fog drifting over the bog would lift and at last she would have a clear day to work. She packed her lunch, filled the thermos with hot, black coffee and climbed into the cab of her truck.

As she drove along the dike that ran the perimeter and between the beds of the bog, something caught her attention. Two figures hunched over, their backs to each other as the man watched her approach and the girl pawed the sandy ground with one foot like a horse anxious to make a break for it.

"Well, now, what have we here?" Jo murmured as she glanced at her watch. She couldn't help wondering when the last time might have been that the girl had been up at this hour. She slowed the truck to a stop several yards from them and took her time gathering her thermos and tools.

"Mornin'," she called as she started toward them.

"Looks like more rain," Daniel said.

"This will burn off by midmorning," she assured him. "Coffee?"

"Not unless you've got a quad venti nonfat no whip mocha in there," the girl grumbled.

"Afraid not, so I'll take that as a no from you. How about you? Plain, old-fashioned drip-brewed caffeine?" she asked, turning to Daniel and holding up the thermos.

"Yes, please. Intravenously, if possible."

Jo laughed. The kid rolled her eyes, hugged herself and moved a little farther away from them. Jo suspected that Jazz didn't want to run the risk that anyone might happen by and think she actually knew these dorks.

After handing Daniel his coffee and getting for herself the car mug she'd filled before leaving the house, Jo turned her attention to the bog.

"Any news from the hospital this morning?"

"I called," Daniel said. "Mom was up and having her breakfast. I have a meeting later with the social worker, but thought I'd get things started here." He jerked his head toward Jazz, who instantly bristled.

"Hello? I am standing not two feet from you. You don't have to talk in code."

"I see you found some work clothes." Jo nodded approvingly at Jazz's outfit of jeans and fleece vest over a flannel shirt that she recognized as belonging to Ella. "Nice boots," she added. Jazz was wearing a pair of military-green galoshes. Her long hair was pulled up in a ponytail and anchored with a baseball cap.

"Dad, could we just get this over with?" the girl muttered, ignoring Jo.

"Ms. Cooper is in charge," Daniel reminded her.

"But it's not her property. She just works for Grandma, and now for you since Grandma is in the hospital."

"Hello? I'm standing right here," Jo said in a perfect imitation of Jazz's earlier protest. "How about we start by assessing the damage?"

Jo worked her way down the side of the dike to the sandy bed below, then knelt to examine several plants.

"Well?" Daniel asked from above her.

"Come see for yourself," she invited, "and bring my helper there with you."

It had been years since Daniel had spent any time working the beds, and yet he was amazed at how quickly things came back to him. The bed had been well prepared—cleared of old growth, spread with sand and leveled. At least, most of it was level. The area where Jazz had gotten stuck looked more like a kid's sandbox excavation site. The cuttings had been evenly distributed and rolled into the sand with a mechanical planter. Except for those cuttings that had been pulled free when Jazz had trampled over several rows.

"I think you can handle it with a few hand tools," Jo said as she climbed back onto the dike and got the required tools from the back of her truck. "You okay here?" she asked.

Nodding, Daniel went to work. "There," he told Jazz once he'd shown her how to level the sand again and was ready to replant the uprooted vines. "Just take that piece and push it back into its place, anchor it down with sand, then go about this far and do the same thing."

Jazz held up the cutting and examined it. "I can't tell which end goes in the ground," she said.

"Doesn't matter. It'll grow either way," Jo said.

"Really? That's weird."

Daniel chuckled as he recalled being only five or six when he'd said almost the same thing to his father. He stood and stretched his back as he gazed down the length of the bed, then looked back at Jo.

"In four or five years, Ella's going to have a far higher yield, at least from this bed," Jo said.

"In four or five years, this land will probably be all filled in with houses, not cranberries," he replied. "It's a pure waste of time, effort and money. Why didn't you talk her out of it?"

"Because this is your mother's life—her livelihood. If I can get her a greater yield from the small acreage she has here, then she'll realize a greater income from the harvest."

Daniel pulled off his cap and ran his fingers through his hair. "Her income comes from Social Security and from me. This is nothing but a hobby—a way of keeping the past alive. Some women get into scrapbooking. My mother raises cranberries."

"Somehow I doubt those ladies who scrapbook ever see checks totaling up to thirty thousand dollars a year for their efforts," Jo muttered as she turned and stalked away.

"Hey," Jazz shouted when Jo passed her, "I just finished repairing that row."

* * *

Ignoring the kid, Jo climbed back onto the grassy dike and went to meet her crew. "Let's finish getting those sprinklers tested," she called.

Could Ella's son have a point? Certainly when Jo had first met the woman, she'd been impressed with Ella's physical strength and sharp mind. Had she seen something in Ella that reminded her of her own mother? Something in the older woman's smile and wisdom had made Jo think. Maybe spending the season with Ella would ease the pain of her mother's death, so unexpected when the porch of a ski lodge condominium her parents had rented for a week had collapsed.

At first the plan had been for her brother Hank to take the job on Nantucket, but then he'd suddenly backed out. "You go, Jo."

"Why? Don't you think I can handle things here?"

"That's not it and you know it," Hank had snapped.

"Then what is it?"

Hank had sighed. "Look, sis, Mom's death was hard on all of us, especially Dad. But you lost more than a parent. You and Mom were more like best friends—sisters. Maybe out there, you can find some peace, some healing."

Jo couldn't argue the point. There were still times when something would remind her of her mother and she would suddenly feel tears leaking down her cheeks. Like now.

She swiped away the tears with the back of her hand and kept working, cleaning out leaves and debris from the last section of sprinkler pipes, then fitting the pieces together while her crew of two did the same down the way. She could hear them talking politics and sports. It reminded her of the way her brothers had kept up a running banter whenever the family was working the bog.

She glanced back toward the farmhouse and cottage.

Back on their farm when she was a kid, her mom would sometimes bring them all lunch, a jug of fresh lemonade on hot afternoons or a thermos of coffee on cold mornings. And up until a few days ago Ella had done the same.

She caught a flash of Jazz's yellow cap and saw Daniel helping his daughter back onto the road. He scanned the beds, obviously looking for Jo, so she waved and put down the pipes she'd been cleaning.

"I'll be back in a minute," she called to her crew.

Daniel met her halfway.

"I think we got it all squared away, but if you see anything more, just let me know."

"I'm sure it's fine," she said as she watched Jazz heading back toward the farmhouse. "For what it's worth, I think you did the right thing. Not only having her show up this morning, but also coming with her, helping her set things right."

"Really?"

Jo was surprised at how uncertain he sounded. Then he laughed. "This parenting thing was a lot easier when she was three."

They had reached the repaired bed and Jo paused to study the results. "Looks like somebody knew what he was doing," she said.

"Yeah, well, Dad always said it was like riding a bicycle. Once you've done it enough you never quite lose the knack of it."

"It's hard for me to imagine you here," Jo admitted. "I mean you and Jazz seem like such…"

"City slickers?"

"Do you ever miss it?"

Daniel stared out over the mature beds to where the men were preparing to test the sprinklers for leaks or clogs they might have missed. "I don't know," he said. "I guess it's been a long time since I gave it much thought."

He bent and picked up the thermos cup of now-cold coffee, tossed the remains onto the ground and screwed the cup back onto the thermos. "Thanks for the coffee," he said. "It was definitely a lifesaver."

"No problem."

The silence stretched long enough to become awkward, and then they spoke at the same time.

"Look, about your mom…" she said.

"I was thinking…" he said.

"Go ahead," they both said, and then grinned.

"You were thinking?" she prompted.

"I was thinking that even if Mom makes a full recovery from this, I need to start making some plans for her future."

"Nantucket is her home," Jo reminded him.

"I know, but I have to be practical. I'm all she's got and I have a business to run in the city, not to mention a rebellious teenager to keep an eye on."

"What are you saying?" Jo felt as if her heart had gotten lodged in her throat.

He frowned and ran his hand over his unshaven jaw. "Just don't go spending any more than you absolutely have to on this season's crop until I can figure things out, okay?"

"Ella hired me to bring in the crop and that's what I intend to do. If you're suggesting that I not do everything in my power to make sure it's a successful crop, then…"

His eyes blazed as he suddenly turned to face her. "Perhaps I should get someone else," he said.

"Perhaps you should talk to your mother before you go around firing the help she hired," Jo replied tersely before heading back to the bog. Just when she thought the guy might be all right, interesting even, he morphed right back into big-city tycoon.

Chapter Five

When Daniel reached the hospital, he learned that his mother had signed the paperwork necessary to go forward with the surgery later that afternoon.

"Mom, we should talk about this."

"There's nothing to discuss. My hip is shot. The doctors can replace it. As I have heard you say on numerous occasions, 'it's a done deal.'"

"Are you scared, Grams?"

It always amazed Daniel that just about the time he thought there might be no hope for his daughter to become more than a spoiled little rich girl, she would show this caring side of her personality.

"I am, a bit," his mother admitted, holding out her hand to Jazz. "Will you pray for me?"

Jazz took Ella's hand between hers and nodded. "Sure. There's a chapel right here in the hospital. We passed it on our way up here."

"And take your father with you—and Jo, if she's around. Can't have too many prayers, right?"

"I'll take care of it," Jazz assured her.

"And now, Jasmine dear, I wonder if you wouldn't mind waiting outside while your father and I talk a little business."

"Sure. I could get you some ice cream."

Ella smiled. "Maybe after the surgery. Right now they've got me on this." She motioned to the intravenous drip on the opposite side of the bed.

"Right. Now I remember. Dad got me ice cream *after* my tonsils came out." She leaned in and kissed her grandmother's cheek. "It's going to be fine, Grams," she said, but her voice broke and she hurried out of the room without saying any more.

"Stay in the waiting room," Daniel called after her. He couldn't help feeling torn between his daughter's need for reassurance and his mother's understandable anxiety as she faced surgery that could possibly have a life-changing outcome. He went to Ella's bedside and took her hand. "Mom, Jazz is right. Everything is going to turn out all right."

"Well, of course it is. Now, stop wasting time and listen to me." She indicated with a nod of her head that he should sit down. "Now then, while I am certain everything will turn out just fine, we need to face facts. I am not a young woman and surgery is—well, surgery."

"Mom…"

"If something should go wrong, the doctor knows my wishes and has my living will on file, so that's not the concern. The concern is what will happen to the farm once I'm gone. I have not spent my entire life working that land and keeping up that place to have you sell it off to some developer, Daniel."

"Do we really need to talk about this now?" he asked with a glance toward the door.

"Jasmine will be fine. She has our resiliency, thank goodness. But that farm is her legacy, Daniel."

Daniel could not imagine Jazz spending any time on

the farm except under duress, and his expression must have said so.

"Oh, right now she thinks the place is the outer banks of never," Ella continued, "but thanks to you and Gloria, she has had an unsettled life. I want her to know that she has this one place that will always be there no matter where she goes. If she never spends another day there, so be it. It's the idea that she has this place called home—and for that matter, so do you."

Daniel stood and paced the small room. "Mom, I know you're nervous about the surgery, but this kind of talk is..."

"Straight talk, young man. Facing realities. Something you used to be quite adept at. God willing, the entire conversation is unnecessary at this time, but if not now...when?"

"If you want to leave Jazz a legacy, then leaving her the farm is fine, but don't tie her to a promise that she won't sell the place. You know what land on this island is worth. Why would you..."

"Because you cannot put a price tag on home," Ella replied as the nurse and an orderly entered the room. "Ah, my escorts have arrived. Give me a kiss, dear, and then go find Jazz."

After kissing Ella's forehead, Daniel walked alongside as the orderly steered the gurney through the hallway to the elevator. "See you in a bit," Ella called gaily as the elevator doors slid shut. Daniel swallowed his own fears and went in search of his daughter.

The crew left after they finished setting up and testing the sprinkler system. Jo was on her own now. She could certainly handle the bulk of the work involved in nurturing and harvesting ten acres of well-established cranberry vines. She stored the tools in the large prefabricated storage shed that stood a hundred yards beyond the farm-house, checked the repaired hybrid plants and then went back to the cottage.

She'd called the hospital earlier, knowing Ella would be awake at dawn. Ella had told her she'd decided to go forward with the hip replacement surgery and asked Jo to pray for her. There was no point in calling the hospital now, she thought as she showered and changed. She wasn't family and the receptionist would be unlikely to give her information about Ella's condition. The surgery should be just getting started.

Why hadn't she given Daniel her cell number and asked him to call?

"Because that would have been the sensible thing to do and there's something about being around that man—and his kid—that seems to make good common sense fly right out the window," she grumbled as she towel dried her short hair.

Fifteen minutes later she was in her truck and on her way to the hospital. She'd stopped once to check Ella's house and found the door unlocked, the kitchen sink filled with dirty dishes and the coffeemaker still on. Shaking her head, she turned off the appliance, washed the dishes and left them to air dry then switched on the outside lights. It would be after dark before Daniel and Jazz returned. She locked the door behind her.

She'd just stepped off the elevator at the hospital when she saw Jazz walking very quickly down the hall. The teen's head was bent, her face obscured by her long hair, but her demeanor exuded obvious distress.

"Jazz?"

The girl paused, glanced back and then kept walking. In that instant Jo saw that she was crying and hurried to catch up with her. "What's happened?" she asked, fighting to keep her voice calm even as her throat tightened with panic. "Did the surgery…"

"They haven't taken her to surgery yet—some delay. She told me…" The girl swallowed a sob, then blurted, "She told me to pray for her."

"Well, that's not a bad idea," Jo murmured as her heart slowed to a more normal beat and she was able to focus all of her attention on the girl. "Come on. I'll pray with you."

Jo took it as a mark of just how frightened the girl was that Jazz did not resist when Jo wrapped her arm around her shoulder and led the way down the hall to the hospital chapel. Inside they took chairs in the front row. Jo looked up at the small stained-glass window while Jazz glanced sideways at her and muttered something indecipherable.

"What?" Jo whispered, in spite of the fact they were the only occupants of the room.

"I don't know how to pray," Jazz said through gritted teeth. "I went to Sunday school when I was a kid, but the 'rents were never big on the church thing."

Jo responded with the first thing that came to mind. "Not even your dad?" After all, she didn't know Jazz's mother, but any son of Ella's would surely have been raised with a strong sense of faith.

"He works most Sundays. You know a hotel is 24/7 year-round." Jazz sounded more like her defensive self. She waited a beat. "So, can you show me how? Grams is counting on me."

Okay, this temporary farming idea was turning out to be a whole lot more complicated than Jo or her brother had ever imagined. What did she know about mentoring a teenage girl? What did she know about teaching anyone how to pray? A person just did it.

"Well, everybody has their own way, I guess."

"So, what's your way?"

"I just sit quietly and think about whatever is on my

mind that needs God's intervention—or that has turned out well because of God's intervention—and then I consider all the ways I've been blessed."

Jazz faced forward, clasped her hands and squeezed her eyes shut. After ten seconds she started tapping one foot impatiently. Then she sighed. "Nothing," she lamented. "Aren't I supposed to feel something?" she asked Jo.

Peace. Reassurance. God's promise that life has purpose and meaning.

Jo reached for the Bible on the table that served as an altar. "Let's try it this way," she said, flipping through the onionskin pages until she found what she wanted, even as she prayed that God would give her the guidance she needed to help this child.

Suddenly she had an idea. "Jazz, do you ever practice yoga?"

"Yeah. So?"

"Come here." Jo moved from the chair to the floor, where she folded her legs in the traditional yoga seated position. Jazz gave her an exasperated look, but followed her lead.

"Now what?"

"Close your eyes," Jo instructed. "Breathe."

In less than a minute the strained lines around the girl's mouth and eyes had smoothed and she was breathing deeply. Jo opened the Bible and in a low voice began reading the Twenty-third Psalm. When she came to the line about walking through the valley of the shadow of death, she hesitated and glanced up.

Tears were leaking from under Jazz's closed lids and her lips were moving. Unaware that Jo had stopped reading, she was going on with the psalm, clearly drawing on a memory from those days when she had attended Sunday school and probably memorized the verses. Matching her words to Jazz's lip-syncing, Jo finished reading the psalm. She waited a beat and then quietly added, "Amen."

After a moment, Jazz's lids fluttered open and she glanced around as if she had forgotten where she was. Then in a voice filled with awe she whispered, "I feel…better."

Jo breathed a silent prayer of thanks and got to her feet. "Good. How about we go find your dad and see how things are going?"

The last thing Daniel expected to see was Jo Cooper coming out of the chapel with Jazz, and for once his daughter wasn't scowling. When he hadn't found Jazz in the waiting room or downstairs in the hospital's coffee café, he remembered that his mother had asked her to pray for her. It had seemed a long shot, but he preferred to think his daughter might have gone to the chapel, rather than entertain his fear that once again she had seen her chance to get back to New York and had run away.

"Dad! How's Grams?"

"They took her up to surgery about twenty minutes ago." Daniel included Jo in the delivery of this news.

"She'll be fine, Dad," Jazz assured him. "Are you okay?"

If he lived to be a hundred, Daniel did not think he would ever get used to the rhythms that guided the teenage mind. One minute his daughter was pure attitude and rebellion, and the next she was the caring young woman he had always hoped she would become.

"Fine, honey. How about we grab some lunch?" Again, he included Jo.

"Why don't the two of you go on to the waiting room and I'll go to the café and bring something up?"

"I'll get it," Jazz said, holding out her hand to Daniel. "Turkey sandwich and water?"

Daniel nodded and handed her a twenty.

"Jo?"

"Oh, just some hot tea," Jo said. "Are you sure you don't want me to come with you?"

"You have to eat," Daniel insisted in a perfect imitation of his mother. "Get two turkey sandwiches and some chips," he told Jazz before adding another five to the money.

"How do you know I'm not a vegetarian?" Jo asked after Jazz had caught the elevator and they were on their way back to the waiting room.

"I don't. Are you? I can go catch Jazz and…"

"Nope. Carnivore," Jo assured him. "And thanks for lunch."

Daniel grinned. "Better hold off on that. Hospital food is usually not exactly fine dining."

"How bad can they mess up a turkey sandwich?" Jo sat down and picked up a magazine while Daniel checked in with the nurse's station.

"No news," he said after returning and taking the seat next to her. "That's good, don't you think?"

"I'm sure of it." Jo resumed flipping through the magazine to cover her own anxiety about Ella. "Your mother is a strong woman. A wonderful woman."

"Yeah. Thanks." Daniel leaned forward, hands dangling between his knees. "Look, whatever you did to help Jazz in the chapel just now, thanks for that."

"She's just worried about Ella. We all are."

"Mom and I had a talk before they took her to surgery." He swallowed. "About what she wanted if things didn't…" He looked toward the window and didn't finish the thought.

Jo laid the magazine aside and gave Daniel her full attention. "From what I know of Ella, she's a practical woman. I expect she's thought a great deal about that, the same way she's given a lot of thought to her future if things go well."

"Planting a whole new bed of hybrids that won't produce for another three years? At her age? How practical is that?"

"Chronological age is a number." She hesitated. "Take you, for instance."

Daniel felt his defenses automatically kick into a higher gear. "What about me?"

"Well, looking at you and having had several opportunities to interact with you these last few days, I'd guess you're what? Mid-forties?"

"I'm thirty-nine," he protested. At least for another couple of months. "Obviously people even in their late twenties tend to view anyone over thirty as ancient."

She burst out laughing. "Late twenties? I wish. Well, actually I don't wish. I wouldn't go back."

He lifted an eyebrow and waited.

"I'm thirty-six," she said and picked up the magazine. "As I said, chronological age is nothing more than a number."

Daniel openly studied her. Well, sure, there were those tiny little laugh lines around her eyes, but otherwise her skin was smooth and firm. A little freckled across the cheekbones and nose but certainly not aged. He scrubbed his own face with one hand and could practically feel its haggardness.

"As you mentioned, it's been a rough few days," he said as if there had been no break in the conversation.

She kept flipping through the magazine.

"Are you going to help me or not?" he asked.

Once again she closed the magazine and placed it with a ragtag stack on the table. "That depends on what you want in the way of help," she replied. "But let's be clear about one thing—I work for Ella. She is also becoming a good friend. I will listen to what you have to say and consider it on its merits, but I will not be part of any scheme to get Ella off this island if she doesn't want to leave."

Daniel had no time to respond to that calmly delivered lecture before Jazz arrived with lunch, just as the doctor entered the waiting room from the opposite direction.

"Everything went fine," he said. "She's in recovery now. Should be back up to her room within the hour." He smiled at Jazz, who was still holding the lunch tray. "That looks good." Then he turned back to Daniel. "I'll stop by later on evening rounds, but if you have any questions or concerns, just ask the nurse to page me."

Then he shook Daniel's hand, nodded to Jo and winked at Jazz as he made his escape. Jazz went to the table by the window and started setting up lunch, but Jo couldn't help noticing that Daniel did not move.

"You okay?"

"They always say that," Daniel muttered. "'Everything went fine,'" he mimicked in a falsetto voice. "Fine for him. What about Mom?"

"One step at a time," Jo said. "But for now Jazz is relieved, and you need to eat."

Jazz was not only relieved. From the look on her face, she was clearly convinced that with the success of Ella's surgery she would be back in the city in a few days. "So, Dad, we can probably leave for the city by the end of the week, right?"

"And leave me to manage the cranberry beds all by myself," Jo protested.

Jazz's head shot up and her eyes flashed with unspoken protest, then softened into relief. "Joke, right?"

"Joke," Jo admitted. "Although I have to say you did a

terrific job repairing the damage to that new bed. Must have some of Ella's gift for nurturing the land."

Jazz picked at her lunch. "One time when I was little," she said after a moment, "I planted a kitchen herb garden for a school project. Remember, Dad?"

"I do," he said. "You kept it on the roof of the hotel."

"Mom was sure she was allergic to the smell of rosemary—or oregano. Maybe it was both."

"Mom was not allergic," Daniel said with a frown.

Jazz laughed nervously. "Yeah, how could she be allergic and go off to study cooking with some big-time French chef in Paris? I mean, those guys use herbs, right?" This comment was directed at Jo as if she were the expert.

"I'm not much of a gourmet cook," Jo replied, "but the right combination of herbs can add flavor to any recipe." Suspecting that the topic of Jazz's mother was upsetting the girl, Jo changed the subject. "Hey, speaking of food, this lunch isn't half-bad for hospital fare." She glanced up at the wall clock. "Why don't you two go on up to Ella's room so you're there when she gets back from recovery. Tell her I'll stop by this evening."

"You're not coming?" Daniel asked.

Jo busied herself with clearing the table. "No. You go on. I have some errands to run and then I need to make some calls." She pulled out one of her business cards and handed it to him. "My cell number is on there. Call me if anything changes."

Daniel took out his wallet to store the card and handed her his business card. "Just in case," he said.

Jazz released a long, dramatic sigh. "I'd give you my number as well, but I don't seem to have a phone."

Grinning, Daniel wrapped his arm around her and pulled her close. "Let's go see Grams. You can plead your case with her."

Jo watched them go and tried to decipher the feelings churning inside her. Feelings of relief that Ella, who had become like a mother to her in just a few short weeks, was out of surgery. Feelings caught up in the constant knot of pain that came with knowing she would never see her own mother again. Feelings of empathy for Jazz, whose mother had apparently gone off to Paris at a time when her daughter needed her here. Feelings of compassion for Daniel, who was caught between his family responsibilities and his own needs. For the first time since meeting him, she felt a measure of charity toward the man. Maybe she could help him after all—not the way he had in mind, but nevertheless, help him find the solution that would work best for him, as well as for Ella.

Chapter Six

Ella spent five days in the hospital and then moved to a rehabilitation center for another month. As soon as she was settled in rehab, Daniel and Jazz left for New York and Jo breathed a sigh of relief. Ella's son and granddaughter had been a distraction from the work she'd been hired to do, and she was anxious to get back to a normal routine.

She started by getting up half an hour earlier and heading into town for breakfast with Ella. The fare was definitely nothing like Ella's home-baked breads and goodies, but they talked about the crop and Ella's therapy and looked forward together to the day when Ella would be home again.

"I understand you took Jazz to the chapel during my surgery," Ella said one morning toward the end of her stay in the rehab unit.

"She was worried about you."

Ella eyed Jo over the rim of her mug of tea. "Thought you'd given up on praying once your mom died."

"I didn't give up," Jo protested. "I just…" Stopped going to church, she thought, because every time I walked through the doors and heard an organ playing it reminded me of her.

"I pray," she mumbled, concentrating on her eggs and overdone bacon.

"I expect Daniel strayed as well," Ella said. "He's always working and he tries to tell me that the weekends can be the busiest times, but I tell him that God doesn't keep regular hours any more than he does."

Jo couldn't help wondering where this was going, but she kept quiet and let Ella ramble on.

"It's Jasmine I worry about. I mean, every child needs a solid base. Daniel has that. His father and I made sure that we were in church every Sunday morning and took the boy to Sunday school." She beamed with motherly pride. "He taught the ten-year-olds his senior year in high school. Those kids adored him. He's a good teacher—knows how to talk their language."

Jo remembered how frustrated and mystified the man had seemed when dealing with his own daughter, but again she didn't comment.

"He should have been a teacher. Running some fancy-shmancy hotel doesn't suit him at all." She popped the last of her biscuit into her mouth and added, "It's the reason he's totally miserable, you know."

"Maybe he's just worried about you, and with his daughter's troubles at school coming at the same time..."

Ella waved away Jo's comment. "Symptoms. No, he chose a life he thought he wanted and once he realized it wasn't for him, he didn't know how to get out of it. He's good at his work—perhaps too good. Always on the phone checking up on things, but I don't say a word. He's a grown man, and in God's own time Daniel will find his way." She winked at Jo. "Maybe God's working on it as we speak."

"I don't understand."

"I fall. Jasmine gets in trouble at school. You're here.

Yes, I would say God has heard my prayers for that son of mine. He's lining up the stars here and I think He has some surprises in store for Daniel—and maybe for you as well."

Jo laughed. "Ella, you are an incurable romantic. You never saw two single people that you didn't think about how they might do together."

"Did I say a word about you being with my Danny? No. That came out of your mouth, which tells me somewhere in that brain of yours you are starting to think about it. Well, keep thinking. Ah, here's my warden."

She looked up and grinned at the muscular young man approaching the table.

"Ready to work out, Mrs. Armstrong?"

"Ready to give you a few more days to torture me and then I am going home, young man."

"Then I'd better work you extra hard these next two days." He grinned at Jo and then wheeled Ella away.

"Think about what I said, Jo," Ella called out.

"See you tomorrow," Jo replied.

On the drive back to the farm it wasn't the ridiculous conversation about Daniel that stayed with her. It was his easy smile and the way he made Jo feel as if she were part of the family. Of course, the very idea that there could ever be the slightest romantic attraction between her and Ella's son was only a figment of Ella's imagination. No, it was Ella's comments on faith that stuck with her.

What would her mother say if she knew that Jo had found one excuse after another to avoid attending services? Even here on the island, where her weekends were virtually free of responsibility. Every time Ella had asked her to come with her and Cyrus Banks to the church they attended in town, she had found some excuse.

Maybe it's time, she thought as she turned down the lane to the farm. In front of the farmhouse was a car with

New York license plates, trunk open and piled with luggage.

They're back, Jo thought and couldn't quite decide if what she was feeling was panic or relief.

Daniel was nowhere in sight but Jazz was leaning against the car. Her lips were moving but Jo saw no one else around and then realized the girl was talking to someone on her cell phone—a phone so tiny it was completely hidden by her long hair. She did not look happy.

Daniel had used the weeks that his mother was in rehab to develop a plan. It was clear to him that she was going to need help over the summer. It was equally clear that, however well the rehab went, it was time they both started seriously planning for the day she could no longer manage alone on the farm.

As for Jazz, Daniel had called Gloria and explained the situation, and while she had been genuinely concerned for Ella, her advice on how to deal with Jazz had stunned him.

"A summer on the farm is exactly what she needs, Danny. Ella has always been such a good influence on her, and the solitude will give her the time she needs to think about her mistakes."

Daniel was not fooled for one minute. The interpretation of this little speech was that Gloria wanted to stay in Paris. So much for motherly devotion, he thought cynically.

Stop it, Daniel admonished as he carried another load of luggage into the house and up the stairs. If Jazz truly needed her Gloria would be here, and you know it. This is about you.

But admitting that didn't help his mood much. "Jazz, get off that phone and give me a hand with this stuff or lose your phone privileges for another two weeks."

The now-familiar sigh escaped her lips as she muttered something to the person on the other end of the phone, snapped the phone closed and slid it into the pocket of her designer jeans.

"How come you brought your car? Usually you just rent one." Her eyes went wide with understanding. "Because we're staying?"

Daniel hauled another suitcase from the trunk and set it on the ground.

"Your grandmother needs us."

"For how long?"

"I'm not sure," Daniel said as he started rolling the luggage toward the house. "But I've made arrangements for Greg to handle things at the hotel for the next six weeks, at least."

He had to admit that Jazz looked like she was modeling for Edvard Munch's painting *The Scream*. And the truth was, for once he understood exactly how she felt.

"This place is beyond boring," Jazz declared the next evening when Jo came to the farmhouse. Ella had asked her to make sure that everything the therapist had suggested had been taken care of in transforming the first-floor den into a bedroom for her.

"I mean, the average age in this outpost seems to be somewhere around fifty," Jazz continued as she watched Jo check off the list the therapist had given her.

"There are people your age," Jo said. "More arriving every day, now that school is out. But there are locals as well. You just haven't met them."

"Ya think? How am I supposed to meet anyone when I'm stuck out here in the boonies?"

"Ella has a bike out in the shed. You could bike into town."

The expression Jazz gave her was nothing short of pure dismay. "Have you seen that bike? It's a grandma bike— a three-wheeler."

"And?"

"I would not be caught dead on something like that."

Jo shrugged. "Just an idea." She rolled up a potentially hazardous throw rug from next to Ella's bed and put it away in the closet. "Where's your dad?"

"He went to the rehab center. Grams is interviewing home-care workers and he wanted to be there. Like she couldn't handle it alone." Jazz sighed. "Sometimes he is so overprotective."

"He's a parent—and an only child. Someday you'll understand."

They worked in tandem for several minutes until Jazz said, "I don't know how he thinks he's going to sell this place. Who would want an old house like this that's not even on the beach?"

Jo forced herself to remain calm. "What makes you think he's planning to sell?"

"We had dinner with his old college friend last week. She's this hotshot real estate broker. When he told her about this place I honestly thought she was going to drool on her food, she was so excited. I don't get it."

But I do, Jo thought anxiously. Once again, she found herself right back in the middle of the debate she'd been having with herself every time she had seen Daniel stroll the property making notes on his BlackBerry. Stay out of it, she prodded herself. This is between Ella and her son.

But every time she sat atop the mower cutting the weeds on the dikes and scanned the acres of pink, starlike cranberry blossoms that surrounded her, she knew she could not stay neutral. This was the last working cranberry farm on the island. There was the preserve, of course, but this farm was a piece of history and Jo hated the idea that some New York Realtor might think nothing of clearing the land, draining the wetlands and putting up rows of cloned vacation houses in its place.

Once Ella is home, we'll work it all out, she reasoned. "That should do it," she announced to Jazz.

"It looks nice," the teenager said. "Maybe some flowers?"

"Great idea. You can pick some and put them in a vase in the morning before she gets home."

"I was thinking more along the lines of ordering a dozen roses from a florist."

"Trust me. Your grandmother will appreciate a natural bouquet that you picked and arranged yourself far more."

Jazz looked skeptical. "If you say so."

The following day, Jo was preoccupied with pollinating the plants for the season. She'd arranged for Cyrus Banks and his grandson, Matt, to deliver the beehives she needed to supplement the wild bees that visited the bog at this time of year.

From the kitchen window at the cottage she saw Cyrus's flatbed truck coming up the road. On the back were seven hives—one for every two-acre bed and two more for good measure, as Cyrus had said. She grabbed her hat and hurried out to meet them.

Matt pulled the truck to a stop and hopped down. "Matt Banks," he said thrusting his hand at her and grinning. "My folks own the market in town, and I work for Grandpa."

"Jo Cooper," she replied, liking the young man at once. "Can you handle the forklift?"

"Yes, ma'am."

Cyrus stepped down from the cab of the truck wearing his beekeeper's garb. "Morning, Jo," he called and then turned to gaze over the bog. "There, there and over there?" He pointed to spots he thought best for the hives.

"Sounds like a plan," Jo agreed.

"You might want to tell that girl there to stand clear until we get the hives in place. Wouldn't want her to get stung in case one of the hives gets juggled or dropped."

"Ah, Grandpa, I'm not going to drop any of them."

"Happens to the best of us."

Jo heard this exchange but did not react. Instead she starting running down the grassy path between beds to where Jazz was standing next to a huge pile of blossoming stems she had just clipped from Ella's best-producing vines.

"What are you doing?" she cried, when, of course, the real question was "What have you done?"

"Picking a bouquet for Grams." Jazz took one look at Jo and added, "It was your idea, although you might have told me I was going to need really small vases."

"I meant flowers—like…" Jo cast her eye over the property and settled on a cluster of white blossoms near the house. "Daisies. Right there outside the back door of the house."

"I like these better," Jazz replied and bent to gather the pile she had created. "They look like wild birds or something."

"Crane heads," Jo murmured automatically while she fought to calm herself. "Did you really need so many?"

Jazz giggled. "I guess I got carried away, but no worries. I'll fill vases and put them all over the house. Grams will think she's walked into a fairyland."

Grams will have a heart attack, Jo thought.

"Hey, who is that?" Jazz's attention was riveted on Matt Banks. He drove the forklift toward them while Cyrus followed with the truckload of beehives.

Jo could definitely see the attraction. Matt was tall and

broad shouldered and he had the kind of shy smile that could definitely set a female heart to buzzing.

In the distance she saw Daniel's car coming down the road. "I'll introduce you later. Here comes your grandmother."

Jazz gathered her bundle of blossoms close to her chest and sashayed her way across the dike toward the house.

"Watch it, Mattie." Jo heard Cyrus bellow and turned in time to see one hive shifting precariously on the end of the forklift as Matt watched Jazz.

An hour later as the last hive was set in place, Jo saw Daniel coming toward them. "Oh, great," she muttered.

But Cyrus Banks pulled off his beekeeper's hat and waved it at Daniel. "Just like you to show up when the work's all done," he teased.

"Mom says come up to the house for lunch," Daniel replied as he grasped the older man's hand between both of his and then turned to shake hands with Matt. "Wow, you've grown," he said, and the boy actually blushed.

"Are you sure Ella's up for company?" Cyrus asked, glancing toward the house.

"Not only is she up for it, she's threatened to throw me out if I don't bring the two of you back. My daughter, Jasmine—Jazz for short—is putting some sandwiches together, and there's some leftover potato salad in the fridge, plus some lemonade if you don't mind store-bought."

"Can't pass up a free meal," Cyrus said. "Matt, put that forklift back inside the shed, then come wash up." He tossed his beekeeper's hat onto the seat of his truck and started following Daniel back to the house.

"You coming, Jo?" Cyrus asked.

"I'll... I've got..." I wasn't invited, she thought.

"Mom's asking for you," Daniel said.

Once again she felt the conflict of emotions that seemed

to grow with her every encounter with Daniel. She wished she could figure out where she stood with him—and why she should care.

"Sure. I'll just wash up and be right there."

Daniel was glad for the buffer of Cyrus Banks's company. On the drive home from the rehab center he had once again broached the subject of selling the farm, and Ella had refused to even discuss the matter. Instead she had acted as if he hadn't even spoken and had turned the tables by trying to convince him to leave Jazz on this land with her for the summer. His mother claimed it would do the girl some real good. He couldn't deny the truth of her words, but he balked because he knew Jazz would revolt at the very notion of being banished to the "boonies" for such an intolerable amount of time. So now he and Ella were clearly at an impasse on both matters.

Over lunch Cyrus and Ella kept everyone entertained with tales of the past—like the time Daniel had upset one of the hives and had to be taken to the hospital.

"Oh, I was so frightened," Ella exclaimed. "Your father kept saying everything would be all right, but you were just a baby—not more than five or six."

"Did you get stung, Dad?" Jazz asked.

"Thirty times," Ella said. She reached over and tousled Daniel's hair. "My brave little soldier."

"Mom," Daniel murmured, but he was grinning as he brushed his hand through his hair to straighten it.

"Yep. That's the day I said to your dad that you were going to be just fine when your turn came to care for the bog," Cyrus boomed. Then, realizing that prediction had never come to pass, he added, "But I didn't count on you falling for some city girl and leaving the island for good."

"Well, we might just have skipped a generation. Jazz is here now," Ella announced.

Daniel saw Jazz shoot him a look of pure desperation.

"Jazz is her mother's daughter," he said with a laugh. "City slicker extraordinaire."

"She's also your daughter," Ella reminded him, and everyone concentrated on their food in the uncomfortable silence that followed.

"Of course," Ella continued after a moment, "she's got a bit of a learning curve to overcome, like not picking the blossoms from the vines just because they're pretty."

"Grams!" Jazz blushed scarlet when she saw Matt looking at her with sympathy.

"Perhaps," Jo said, "she wanted to bring you those blossoms so you would feel more a part of things until you have a chance to get back on your feet and come out to the bog yourself."

Daniel thought Jazz might actually hug Jo, and he couldn't help feeling grateful to the woman for the way she'd stood up for his daughter.

Ella was immediately contrite. She reached over and covered Jazz's hand with hers. "Oh honey, that's just so sweet. Thank you." She leaned back and closed her eyes for a moment.

"Mom? You okay?"

"Just a little tired. If you will all excuse me, I'll go lie down for a bit."

All three men at the table were on their feet in an instant. Daniel and Cyrus hovered around Ella as she used her walker and made her way down the hall to her converted bedroom. Jo started clearing the table.

"Is Grams all right?" Jazz asked as soon as Daniel and Cyrus returned to the kitchen.

"Right as rain," Cyrus assured her. "How about you let

this grandson of mine show you his favorite fishing hole? We've got all the gear in the truck. Planned to stop off on our way home."

"I don't know much about fishing," Jazz said shyly.

Cyrus laughed. "Not much to know, and the truth is that you'd be letting me off the hook." Everyone laughed at the pun and Jazz glanced at Daniel for permission.

"If you want to," Daniel said, thinking that the last thing he had ever thought he would see was the day his daughter went fishing. "You do understand that out here on the island we use live bait?"

Jazz shuddered.

"I'll bait your hook," Matt told her. "Come on. It'll be fun."

Jazz looked down at her outfit. "Am I dressed okay?" To Daniel's surprise this question was directed at Jo, who seemed a little baffled to be asked.

"You might want some older shoes—ones you can get wet. And maybe a pair of cutoffs and a T-shirt. And a hat. The sun's pretty strong."

"You change while I take Grandpa home and get my bike. Meet you back here in half an hour, okay?" Matt asked.

"Okay. Sure."

But Daniel could see something was not right, and as soon as Matt and Cyrus left he turned to Jazz. "You don't have to go if you don't want to, honey."

"No, I want to go."

Daniel glanced at Jo as if to ask, Any idea what's going on here?

"Jazz? Matt's bike? It's a motor scooter," Jo said, and Daniel saw his daughter's face light up.

"I have to change," she announced and took off for her room upstairs.

"Translation?" he said once Jazz had left the room.

"We had this conversation about her maybe using Ella's

three-wheeler to get out and around and meet some other kids. I expect she had visions of pedaling along next to Matt and looking—in her words—like a total dork."

"But she didn't say…"

"She didn't have to. It was all right there in her eyes."

Daniel found himself studying Jo Cooper's eyes. They were as green as the beds of vines outside the kitchen window. "Mom wants Jazz to spend the summer here with her," he confided as he picked up a dish towel and dried the dishes she was washing.

"Could be a win-win situation."

"How so?"

"Ella has company and gets to know her granddaughter better. Jazz stays out of trouble—hopefully. And you can get back to work and check in on weekends."

They worked in silence for several minutes. Daniel spread the damp towel over the dish rack while Jo wiped out the sink. "You don't think it's best to move Mom to New York?"

"It doesn't matter what I think. The only thing that matters is what Ella thinks."

"Still, I'm interested in what you think. If this were your mother…"

The look that flashed across her features told him he had struck a nerve.

"I would do everything in my power to make sure that she lived her life where and how she wanted, no matter what I might think was better for her."

And before he could say anything more, she was out the door and on her way out to the bog.

Chapter Seven

Jo spent the remainder of the afternoon in the bed farthest from the house. She worked her way through the bog, pulling weeds and checking for any early signs of pest infestation. She reveled in the warmth of the sun and the salty scent of the breeze off the ocean. And, as was her habit, she talked aloud to God.

"Was it a mistake to come here after all? Maybe I should have insisted that Hank come and I take care of the customers on the mainland."

She thought of her mother, of all the days like this one when the family had gathered for a meal and then gone out together to work the bog. She thought of the times when she was a teen and some boy had caught her fancy and how her mother had understood, while her father and brothers had found the situation cause for teasing.

"Jazz Armstrong is nothing like me," she argued. "And I don't know the first thing about being a mother, even if she does need a mother's attention more than anyone I've ever seen."

But, she thought, there's this instinct within me that wants to nurture her, to protect her, to help her find her way.

Her heart went out to Daniel. Between the demands of his work and Jazz's mother taking off for Europe, all on top of the crisis with Ella, he certainly had enough on his plate. It seemed to Jo that perhaps if Jazz had a friend—an adult friend—she might become part of the solution rather than one more problem Daniel had to manage.

She heard a car engine and shaded her eyes as she looked back toward the house. A strange car had just pulled into the driveway. Probably the home-care worker.

"Good. Ella will have the help she needs and I can concentrate on the job I came here to do."

And yet, she thought, I've come to care for Ella as more than an employer, more than a friend.

"I need a break," she announced to the heron observing her carefully as they made their parallel tracks through the bog. The bird took flight. "Yeah, catch you later," Jo called as she climbed onto a dike and started back toward the cottage.

By the time she got back to the cottage, Daniel's car was gone, and she'd seen Matt and Jazz ride off shortly after she'd started the weeding. The home-care worker's car was still parked outside the house, so Ella was in good hands.

Jo stood in her kitchen with the refrigerator door open and tried to come up with something for her supper. Not that there weren't choices, but nothing appealed to her. The idea of cooking a meal and then settling down in front of the television seemed pathetic.

"Go to town," she instructed herself. "Be with people other than the Armstrong family. Ella's home. The crisis is past. Now get back to normal."

After showering and changing, she left the porch light on and climbed into her truck. It sputtered out twice but then caught, and she waved to the figure in Ella's kitchen window as she passed the farmhouse on her way to the main road.

With the windows down and the wind whipping her short hair, she felt more carefree than she had in weeks. In town, she pulled into a rare vacant parking space and walked up Main Street and down Federal, pausing to window-shop. She bought a mystery novel Ella had mentioned she wanted to read, and at the same time picked up a fashion magazine the clerk assured her was popular with teens like Jazz.

Outside a local pizza place she ran into an old friend from high school who was vacationing on the island with a group of fellow teachers. They persuaded her to join them and it was after eleven by the time they parted ways.

As Jo walked the deserted streets back to her truck she couldn't help smiling. *Thanks, God. This is exactly what I needed. Good food, friends and conversation. Definitely feeling like my old self.*

But her spirits plummeted when she turned the key and this time the truck didn't even sputter. "Come on," she urged, and tried it again, but she didn't need a mechanic to tell her the thing had finally died.

She climbed down and considered her next move. It was at least a six-mile hike back to the farm, not that she couldn't do it, but for some reason this was the night she'd chosen to wear her one and only pair of heels. She could call her friend. They had exchanged cell numbers, but it was so late.

Down the block she saw a figure coming her way—a man and he was whistling. "Please have a car and jumper cables," she whispered as she prepared to call out to him. "Hey! Hello!"

The whistling stopped, as did the man.

"Jo?"

"Daniel?" The automatic flip-flop her heart did these days every time she saw him or heard his voice gave her a familiar jolt of pleasure.

Probably no jumper cables, if she had to guess, but at least she could catch a ride.

"Is everything okay?" Daniel could see that it wasn't. Why would the woman be standing on a deserted street at this hour if things were just fine?

She kicked at the front tire of her truck. "It's the battery. I know I need a new one but I'd hoped to make it through the summer. Can I catch a ride back to the farm?"

"Of course, but…you're just going to leave it here?"

"Unless you've got jumper cables?"

Daniel shook his head.

"Well then, I don't have a lot of choice. I'll call the local cops and let them know it's not the abandoned wreck it appears to be and then catch a ride with Matt Banks tomorrow morning to come get it hauled to a mechanic."

"Sounds like a plan, but I hope you're up for a hike. My car is several blocks away. I had forgotten what an adventure parking in this town can be in high season."

Jo laughed as she retrieved the book and magazine she'd bought for Ella and Jazz and fell into step with him. "I can't imagine that parking in Manhattan is much easier."

"You've got a point. So you had some shopping to do?"

"Impulse buys. I just decided to get out for a bit. Ran into some old friends and had dinner. Serendipity. How about you?"

"Between Mom, Jazz and the home-care woman, I was feeling a little outnumbered." He grinned. "I thought I'd take the opportunity to check out some of the landmark hotels here on the island. As long as I'm here. It always helps to see what others are doing and how I might be able to apply that to the services we offer at the Barrington."

"Ella says you're always working."

"Yeah, I get that a lot from the women in my life," he

admitted. "Jazz has certainly implied that her mother and I are at least partially to blame for her troubles at school."

"Are you?"

Daniel's step faltered at the direct question. "I have a business to run, and her mother…" He paused, not wanting to sound quite so defensive.

"Sorry. That's really none of my business," Jo said. "I mean, what do I know about raising a child? In our house, there were seven of us, so maybe that's different. Certainly both of my parents worked. Mom was a teacher and Dad had the farm to manage, plus serving on the local town council."

Daniel seized the opportunity to turn the spotlight away from his parenting skills and on to her. "Mom tells me your mother died recently. I'm sorry."

"Thanks. It's been harder than I expected for me to grasp the fact that she's gone forever. In so many ways we were more like best friends and I miss her terribly. But you understand. Ella told me your father's death was also unexpected."

Daniel did not meet her eyes. "Some would say he worked himself to death."

"And what would you say?"

"To my way of thinking he probably couldn't have chosen a better way to go. He was tending the bog and looking forward to a bumper crop." He smiled at her. "He would have been pleased with the work we're doing."

His compliment was so unexpected and gave her such a rush of pleasure that she had no words. She released a long sigh and looked down the street. "Where did you say you had to park? If we keep going, we'll be back to the farm."

"One more street. Just next to that last wharf," he assured her. "I thought you farm girls were in shape."

"We are. Wanna race the rest of the way?" And she took off, her high heels clicking on the pavement.

"Hey, no fair," he called as he ran after her, caught up and then sprinted the last ten yards to reach the car at the same time she did. "Tie," he announced, his breath coming so hard and fast that the one-syllable word was a struggle.

"Not so fast, hotshot." To his surprise, she took hold of his hand, extended his index finger to match her own, then sighed. "I knew I shouldn't have trimmed my nails. Okay, tie."

He couldn't help noticing that she was barely breathing hard. He also couldn't help noticing the way their hands fit and the warmth he felt transferring from her palm to his.

"For such a petite lady, you have unusually long fingers," he observed, not wanting to break that contact.

"Next time I'll take you on in a game of one-on-one basketball," she said, and then reached for a paper under the windshield wiper. "You got a ticket. In light of the tie race and the fact you rescued me, I'll split it with you."

"No way. I'm fighting this. I was…"

"Parked in a block where the residents have managed to get parking restricted after six o'clock," she said, pointing to a sign farther down the way.

He fingered the ticket as he stared at the sign. "Well, in light of the fact I already have a ticket, I don't suppose you'd be interested in backtracking a couple of blocks and having a cup of coffee with me at that café at the end of the wharf?"

"It's almost midnight," she protested.

"Early for us city types."

"Late for us farm girls. And coffee? I'll be up the rest of the night and useless tomorrow."

"Ever hear of decaf? And what's so pressing about tomorrow? Seems to me the sprinklers are in place, the bees are humming along and the weeding is under control.

From where I'm standing you've got ten acres of happy cranberry blossoms out there just doing their thing."

Laughter and soft jazz drifted across the wharf. The night was balmy and the bay was calm. Jo was tempted.

"Help me out here," he urged. "The truth is I'd like to grab just one more hour before I have to face the looming problems back there at the farm."

"One cup," she said.

"Two at most," he agreed and took her hand as they set off down the planked wharf.

Outside the café Jo pulled two wooden chairs closer together to face the water while Daniel got their coffee.

"Careful. It's really hot," he said, handing her a large white earthenware mug spewing steam into the night air.

They each took a moment to settle in, to allow the coffee to cool and to breathe in the salt air.

"So what problems are looming, exactly?" she asked.

She expected him to laugh. Instead he took a moment to blow on his coffee and then take a swallow.

"Well, let's see, the list includes my daughter, my mother, my ex-wife…you."

"Me! You barely even know me."

"Fair enough. Let's remedy that. Let's see, I believe you earned a degree in business."

"A master's in business," she corrected.

"Pardon me. And while you were doing that, did you make time for a life? Play sports? Have dates? Get engaged?"

"I had a couple of what you might call serious relationships—one that was headed for the altar."

"What happened?"

Jo shrugged. "I got cold feet." When he didn't seem to know what to say, she added, "Oh, yeah, and I played field hockey and was state champ in archery." She pantomimed shooting an arrow.

Daniel gave a low whistle. "Archery, huh? Let's put you on the potential looming problem side of the page."

"Let's don't put me on the page at all. I'm just hired help, like the woman caring for Ella. And by the way, I think you may be overdramatizing the problems you think you have with Jazz and Ella."

"How so?"

Jo curled her legs beneath her and turned to face him. "Jazz is finding her way. Teens are going to challenge authority—test the waters to see just how strong the rules are. If you cave, then she has her answer. From what I gather she fully expected you to cave when you came up to school to get her."

"Is that what she told you?"

"Actually, what she said was, 'If only it had been Mom who came to school.' I took that to mean that she felt things would have gone easier for her—at least in her view."

Daniel gave her the digest version of what had happened. "Do you think I did the wrong thing? Not standing up to the administration, I mean?"

"I have no idea. I suspect that Jazz gives you a certain grudging respect for not throwing your weight around."

"It's her grandfather who has the weight," Daniel corrected.

"You work for him?"

"I did. When Gloria—Jazz's mother—and I divorced, I got the one hotel as a kind of consolation prize."

"In exchange for what?"

"No exchange. Just Gloria's way of showing her appreciation for me not making a big thing of the divorce." He stared out over the water as a breeze rippled the surface.

"Gloria is the original material girl—the only way she knows to express her feelings is through giving some major gift."

"That's sad." Jo was uncomfortable hearing about Daniel's ex-wife, so she changed the subject. "And Ella? Why is she on the list?"

"She's almost seventy-five years old, Jo. Be realistic. How long do you honestly think she can manage alone in that house, not to mention the farm itself?"

"Seems to me she thought of at least part of that when she decided to hire me this season. She may not be as oblivious to her circumstances as you think, Daniel."

"And what if she'd fallen and fractured that hip in the dead of winter—before you came on the scene?"

Jo couldn't help smiling. "Come on, Daniel, you must know that Cyrus checks on Ella every single day—sometimes twice a day. And she has her friends at church and…"

"But it's so isolated out there and Cyrus isn't getting any younger, either."

Jo drained the last of her coffee in an attempt to control her irritation. It didn't work. "So, you think dragging her off to the city where she knows no one would help?"

"She knows me." He flung the remains of his coffee into a nearby planter and stood up.

"She does at that, and you'll be working seventy to eighty hours a week while she does what?"

He started to speak but couldn't seem to find the words. Finally he settled on, "Do you want a second cup or not?"

"Not," Jo replied. "If you don't mind, I'd like to get some rest. I know you think the berry vines are doing fine on their own but, call me old-fashioned, I just want to make sure."

This time the walk to the car was silent. He opened the door for her and then retrieved the ticket from under the windshield wiper on his way to the driver's side. Inside he reached across and stashed it in the glove compartment, his arm accidentally brushing her knee as he did.

"Sorry," he muttered as he started the engine.

And Jo couldn't help wondering if the apology was for touching her or for the argument they'd just had. She couldn't help hoping that he felt the same spark she did whenever they happened to touch. But if he was apologizing for losing his temper, then might that mean he was beginning to care? Either way she promised herself that she was going to stay out of it. This was his life, his daughter, his mother. She was just there for the season—a farmer raising ten acres of cranberries. Possibly the land's last crop.

Her good mood, restored by a night of shopping and seeing old friends, wavered with the realization that Daniel Armstrong believed he was doing the best he could for his daughter and his mother. And the fact that she thought he was on a path to make an enormous mistake with both of them didn't matter a bit.

Jazz was still up when Daniel passed her room on his way to bed. "Hey, it's pretty late," he said, then noticed her bed strewn with discarded sheets of yellow legal paper as she scribbled furiously on the remainder of a pad. "What are you working on?"

"I just realized tonight that Grams is going to be seventy-five years old on her birthday." She said this with the kind of awe that only a sixteen-year-old can. "We have to have a party—a major party."

"That's not a bad idea." Daniel sat on the edge of the bed and scanned some of her discards. On one was a drawing of a sparkling diamond.

"Get it? Seventy-five is the diamond year?"

"How do you know that?"

"Dad, I do sometimes go to class and read stuff. Queen Victoria had this enormous celebration after she'd been queen for seventy-five years, and look here…" She pulled out one of her fashion magazines from a stack by her bed and flipped to a page. "Here's a list of all the symbols for wedding anniversaries, and see? Seventy-five equals diamond. So, a birthday must also be diamond, right?"

"Okay, so the theme is diamond jubilee."

Jazz laughed and started scribbling again. "Jubilee! I love it. Her birthday's the week after the Fourth of July, so if we have the party on the Fourth, we can tie the whole thing into fireworks and stuff right here on the island. Matt says that they do awesome fireworks, and his mom is a caterer and he—"

"I take it the fishing trip with Matt went well?"

Jazz screwed up her nose. "Yuck! Have you ever tried to take one of those things off the hook? They are so squirmy and slimy." She actually shuddered.

"But you had a good time with Matt?"

"Yeah, and he introduced me to some of his friends. There's this one girl who is training for the Olympics. I mean, how cool is that?"

"Pretty cool," Daniel said, but he was not thinking about Matt's friend. He was thinking about Jazz and how this was the first time in a very long time that he had seen her so caught up in something, so interested in others. He handed the papers back to her and stood up. "Get some sleep and we'll talk more about this tomorrow."

"Dad? Do you think it would be okay to ask Jo to help us? I mean, Matt thinks…"

Daniel could not get over how, after just one afternoon with the boy, Jazz's conversation was already peppered liberally with "Matt says" and "Matt thinks." He seemed like a nice enough kid. Still, he was wary of Jazz getting caught up in some summer romance that might well end before the summer did if he could persuade his mother to return to New York with them.

"Dad?"

He rubbed his eyes and yawned. "What was the question?"

"Jo?"

Yeah. Jo.

"I don't know. She's pretty busy."

"Matt says the cranberries practically raise themselves right now—I mean, unless there's some weather thing like drought or frost or something. He thought we could hold the planning meetings at her cottage so Grams wouldn't catch on to the surprise."

"You and Matt are going to plan this together?"

"And you and his grandfather and Jo, of course." She tapped her pen against the pad. "I wish Mom could be here. The one thing she's practically an expert at is planning something like this."

"Don't get carried away," Daniel said, thinking of some of the blowout charity events Gloria had planned and executed in Manhattan. "This is your Grams, not some high-society blue blood."

"Dad! I know that. So, can I ask Jo to let us meet at her place or not?"

"Sure. Ask her," he said and kissed the top of Jazz's head. "Now, go to bed." He took the pen and pad from her and pulled the covers over her as she scooted down into them. Then he switched off the light.

"We'll need a band," he heard her mutter sleepily as he closed the door.

Chapter Eight

Jo had to look twice to recognize the girl running along the dike and waving. But it was Jazz, all right, her face wreathed in a smile, her hair pulled up in a ponytail that swung like a pendulum behind her. She was wearing cutoff jeans, a T-shirt and sandals. And Jo had to check to make sure she was the only other person around before she realized that Jazz was waving to her. She waved back and waited.

"Hi," Jazz said breathlessly as she slowed to a walk. "Got a minute?"

"Sure. What's up?"

"It's Grams." Jazz took a long moment to steady her breathing before continuing, and Jo's heart flew to her mouth.

"She hasn't fallen again?"

"No. It's her birthday. I mean it will be on the seventh of next month and she's going to be seventy-five. So Matt and I—and Dad—think this calls for a major party."

"Jazz, I think that's a lovely idea."

"So you'll help us?" she asked brightly.

"Any way that I can, but…"

"Great. We need your place for the meetings. Tonight at seven-thirty? That's about the time the home-care person helps Grams with her shower and gets her all settled in to watch television or play some cards with her and such. Grams is usually asleep by nine."

So you could meet in the farmhouse at nine, Jo thought.

As if she'd read Jo's mind, Jazz said, "Of course, I guess we could meet at the house, but what if she wakes up and wants to come into the family room and wants to know what's going on?"

"You're right. The cottage is yours. I'll just clear out, for what? A couple of hours?"

"Clear out?" Jazz looked confused, then the light dawned. "No. We need you there. I'm pretty much a novice at planning something like this, although my mother is awesome, so maybe it's in the genes. But I definitely need another woman's opinion. I mean, if we leave it to Dad and Matt and his grandfather we're likely to end up with hot dogs on the grill and some dorky accordion player or something."

"Well, if you think I can help…"

"As Dad would say, don't sell yourself short. I mean, Grams told me you have six brothers—two sets of twins. I'm guessing your mom had to have come up with some pretty creative ideas for all those birthday parties." She took off at a lope, waving as she went. "Have to meet Matt. See you at seven-thirty!"

Jo went back to her work, moving slowly through each bed of vines, lost in the memories Jazz had stirred.

Birthdays. Parties.

Her mother had indeed created magical celebrations— each individually designed to celebrate the unique personality of the child. Each child got a celebration week. The twins each got their own week and separate parties.

"They are twins—not joined at the hip," her mother would protest when her friends chastised her for going to so much trouble. For Jo, she had designed parties to fit whatever her only daughter's interests were that year.

Jo lifted a dark green vine stem to examine for signs of pest infestation and stared instead at the shadowy cavern beneath it. She remembered the year when she was six and deeply into believing in things like magical fairies and elves and such. That year her mother had stayed up all night and turned their backyard into a wonderland of tiny fairy dolls holding tea parties beneath the umbrella of a May apple plant. And swinging from the branches of the arbor of grapevines that formed the entrance to the garden had been an entire orchestra of elf dolls her mother had made from scraps of fabric and leather she kept in her sewing room. Each doll was playing an instrument.

Jo shook herself back to the present as she felt a drop of moisture hit her thumb and bounce onto a leaf. She looked up at a cloudless blue sky and only then realized the drop was not rain but a tear so perfectly formed that it had fallen whole instead of winding its way down her cheek.

She heard the putter of Matt's motor scooter and looked up in time to see Jazz climb on behind him. The two teens waved to someone on the porch as they took off, and Jo saw that Ella had come out to sit for a while.

Maybe a party for Ella was one way she could honor he own mother's memory. "Pay it forward," her mom had always said.

Daniel was both relieved and surprised at the change in Jazz. He had never quite gotten used to the ability of a teenager to change seemingly overnight, but if he'd had any doubts about his daughter's most recent transformation, they were set to rest when he and Jazz went grocery shopping and ran into a couple of Jazz's classmates from boarding school.

"Hey, how are you?" one girl said, her face carefully arranged in a mask of sympathy so convincing that, for a moment, Daniel thought he might have overlooked some tragedy in his daughter's life.

"Great," Jazz replied, and Daniel noticed that while the smile on his daughter's face was genuine, the other girl's expression was suspect. Something about the way her eyes kept darting around to check out who else might be in the store. "Dad, you remember Cassie and Sasha," she added.

"Good to see you," Daniel said as he shook hands with each girl. "Are you visiting here with your families?"

"Yes," the one called Cassie replied and turned her attention back to Jazz. "The 'rents have been coming here for like the last decade or something. *Très* boring."

Her friend Sasha nodded. To Daniel's shock Jazz laughed.

"Hey, my family's been here for like an entire century or something, right, Dad?" Cassie and Sasha once again assumed the expressions of abject sympathy for what they obviously assumed was Jazz's suffering. Jazz seemed oblivious. "Are you going to be here over the Fourth? Because we're planning like this giant birthday blowout."

"Oh, that sounds like fun," Sasha gushed.

Cassie was more cautious. "It's your birthday?"

"Not mine. My grandmother's. She's like an icon on the island and she's going to be seventy-five. Isn't that awesome?"

Daniel thought that if either girl's smile had been drawn any tighter their glossy lips would have disappeared altogether. "I don't know. Mom said something about maybe going to Ireland for July," Cassie said. "Let me get back to you." She gave Jazz air kisses at either cheek and waited impatiently for Sasha to follow her lead. "Nice seeing you, Mr. Armstrong."

After they'd scurried away, Jazz stood there for a

moment. "You know what's weird? At school Cassie and Sasha shared the suite with me, and I just realized that this is the first time I've heard from either of them."

"Well, I did take away your computer and phone there for a while," Daniel reminded her.

"You didn't turn off my e-mail, voice mail or text messages," Jazz replied as she guided the cart down the aisle and started selecting snacks for the planning meeting. "Ooh, Dad, check out these napkins with the fireworks design. Should I get them now or wait until we plan the party?"

Dan tossed three packages of various-size napkins into the basket. "Better get them now. If you change your theme we can always return them."

"Good plan," Jazz agreed, and consulted her list as she steered the cart to the cheese aisle and seemed to ignore the fact that her two classmates were still standing outside the store, now whispering and laughing. Dan didn't know how teens handled such things these days, but when he was an adolescent he would have been insecure enough to assume the girls were laughing at him.

"You okay?" he asked after catching up with Jazz.

Her eyes flickered toward the window for an instant. She shrugged. "Disappointed, I guess." Then she glanced at Daniel and grinned. "Hey, don't look so worried. It's not Armageddon. Somehow I will survive. Brie or Gouda? Matt likes Gouda."

Daniel tossed one of each into the cart and then hugged Jazz and planted a kiss on her forehead. "I love you, kid," he murmured.

"Dad!" she protested as she pulled away and glanced around. "You're embarrassing me." But Daniel saw that she was smiling as she pushed the cart on to the cracker aisle.

* * *

Jo watched as Daniel brought in three bags of groceries and set them on the counter in her kitchen. "Just how many people are on this committee?" she asked.

"You, me, Matt, Jazz and maybe Cyrus—five," he replied, counting on his fingers. "Why?"

"Looks more like enough for a small army division."

"Yeah. We got a little carried away, but as Jazz says, we'll have plenty for the rest of the meetings—whatever that means." He started taking things from bags and storing them in the refrigerator and pantry, moving around the small kitchen as if he'd lived there all his life. "Surely we can wrap this thing up tonight and she and Matt can pull it together."

"Where is Jazz?"

"She went up to the house so Mom wouldn't wonder what she was doing down here with you."

"And you," Jo reminded him.

"Mom will assume I'm trying to tell you how to manage the crop. She gave me a lecture just yesterday about letting you handle things, and reminded me it's been several years since I was even around except to help Dad with the harvest."

"Look, I'm really sorry—about last night. It's not my place to give you advice and I…"

"No, I'm the one who's sorry. You brought up a good point about Mom being isolated there in the city. I was checking around on the Internet last night and they have these senior communities—even in Manhattan. I thought I'd check into those and see what they're like."

Jo bit her lip to stem any comment she might make about that idea. "How's Ella doing with her rehab?" she asked instead.

Daniel shook his head in amazement. "She's incredible. I mean, you can see what it takes out of her. The pain has to be intense, especially when the therapist is working on her, but she just keeps at it."

Jo smiled. "That's Ella. She's a fighter."

"Like you?"

Jo turned to find him studying her as if seeing her for the first time. She felt the heat rise to her cheeks and decided the safest course was humor. "Hey, when you're the only girl among six older brothers, survival becomes second nature."

"Well, I'd better get back up to the house. See you later?"

"Seven-thirty," she agreed. After a mock salute that made him smile, she added, "Hey, Daniel, this party? It's a terrific idea and I really appreciate the chance to be a part of it."

"Better hold that thought. If I know my daughter, this thing could take on a life of its own and we may all regret agreeing to help." He started to go and then came back. "On the other hand, just so you don't get the wrong idea, let me tell you what happened in town today."

He leaned against the cottage door and told her about the encounter with Jazz's classmates. "She was so incredibly mature about it. I was ready to smack the two of them, but she just took it in stride."

"I'm beginning to realize that, first impressions aside, Jazz is a pretty special person," Jo said.

And, she thought, so is her father.

"Okay," Jazz announced to the group, "I e-mailed Mama and she sent me the following list of things we need to address."

Having volunteered to take notes for the meeting, Jo leaned forward, but she could not help noticing the expression of wariness that crossed Daniel's face.

"Let's just remember that this is a small party for Grams, honey—not a charity ball at the Met."

Jazz rolled her eyes and continued. "First there's the venue."

"Here on the farm, right?" Matt asked.

"Not necessarily. We need to see what's available. After all, it might be best if we hold the event somewhere else, since we want it to be a surprise."

"Next?" Cyrus prompted.

"Theme," Jazz announced and waited for Jo to write that down. "Food. Entertainment. Guest list. Invitations. Color scheme. Décor. Favors. Time line."

"Anything on your mother's list about a budget?" Daniel asked wryly. He was beginning to envision a significant outlay of money for this little shindig.

"Dad!" Jazz cleared her throat. "Let's start with the theme because that will impact everything else."

"Seems to me the theme is Ella's seventy-fifth birthday," Cyrus drawled.

"Her diamond birthday," Jazz corrected.

"We could build the theme around that—diamonds," Jo suggested and was rewarded with Jazz's beaming smile.

"Whoa!" Daniel held up his hands as if to stop an oncoming car. "Mom is a pretty no-fuss kind of woman. I don't think she'd be comfortable with bling."

"Oh, Dad, we're not talking about actual diamonds. Come on, everybody, let's brainstorm. Besides the gem, what is a diamond?"

"A geometric shape," Matt said. "We could do the invitations in a diamond shape. Hey, Grandpa and I could cut some plywood sheets into diamond shapes to use for the tabletops."

"That's brilliant," Jazz crowed. "What else?"

"If we could find pictures of Ella through the years, we

could frame them in diamond-shaped frames. We could cut the frames out of mat board in colors to match whatever color scheme we choose," Jo suggested.

"Write that down," Jazz instructed. "Come on, people, what else? Dad? Mr. Banks?"

Cyrus shrugged. "Sounds like you two ladies have this thing under control."

"Dad?"

"Well, if we switch over to the number seventy-five, maybe we could do something with that—like seventy-five balloons or seventy-five roses or…"

"Seventy-five paper lanterns lighting the venue," Jazz added. "Are you getting all this?"

Jo nodded as she scribbled down ideas.

"Okay, moving on. Color scheme?"

"Her birthday's so close to the Fourth, so red, white and blue?" Matt suggested.

"Not for Mom," Daniel said. "Her favorite colors have always been cranberry red and forest green."

Jo couldn't help thinking that the fact that he remembered such a trivial detail was pretty special. "So deep reds and greens," she repeated as she added that to her notes.

"There's a new paper goods store in town," Matt volunteered. "Maybe Jazz and I could go there."

"Or we could make the invitations," Jo suggested.

For the first time Jazz looked skeptical. "I don't know. I mean, we want this to be really nice."

"Honey, handmade can be pretty special," Daniel said. "Besides, it suits your grandmother."

"I could make up a couple of samples and see if you like them," Jo offered.

"Okay." But Jazz sounded anything but convinced.

"And you just leave the entertainment to me," Cyrus announced. "There's a terrific little local band that Ella likes."

"Do they have a CD?" Jazz asked, her voice starting to waver as the group took on a life of its own.

"They made a couple of records that did pretty well," Cyrus said.

Jo watched Jazz take in the idea of record versus CD and calculate the age of Cyrus's band. "Well, Cyrus, why don't you ask if you can borrow one of their albums. There's an old phonograph here in the cottage and we could listen to their music at our next meeting."

"Sounds like a plan," Cyrus agreed and Jazz started to breathe again.

"Okay then, Dad, how about you and Mr. Banks come up with the guest list. Jo's going to work on the invitations, so Matt and I can start…"

"Checking out venues?" Matt suggested.

"Perfect. Shall we meet again at the end of the week?"

"Works for me," Cyrus said, and stood up. "So, if the meeting's adjourned, I'll get on my way. Don't like driving much after dark these days."

"I can drive you, Grandpa."

"No, you and this young lady probably want to get a head start on that venue thing. Don't keep her out past her curfew," he instructed as he leaned down to kiss Jo's cheek, then shake Daniel's hand and retrieve his battered straw fedora from a hook by the door.

"Are you okay with that, Dad? I mean, is it okay if Matt and I take a ride into town?"

Daniel checked his watch. "Ten o'clock curfew," he said, directing the comment to Matt, not Jazz.

"Yes, sir." And the two teens were out the door before Daniel could change his mind.

"Let me help," Daniel offered when he saw Jo gathering the remains of their snacks.

"I can get it."

He picked up the glasses, dumping leftover liquids into a single glass so he could carry them all. "I used to work busing tables during the summer," he said.

"Is that where you met your wife—ex-wife?"

Now, Jo thought, there's your basic smooth transition. What is the matter with me? But the truth was that from the minute Jazz had presented her mother's party list, Jo had been looking at Daniel differently. He'd been married and his ex-wife was still a part of his life—at least when it came to their daughter. As usual, Jo's curiosity had overpowered her common sense.

"Sorry. None of my business," she muttered as she bent to store the leftover cheese in the small refrigerator.

"As a matter of fact, Gloria and I did meet here on the island. I had just finished my master's in business and had come back here for what I saw as my last summer of freedom before buckling down to a real job."

Well, he seems okay with talking about it, Jo thought. "And Gloria?"

"Her parents had just bought one of the old beachfront properties, torn down the home that had been there since before World War One and built...well, something bigger." He chuckled. "The locals were pretty up in arms about it."

"How so?"

"Part of the mystique of a place like Nantucket is preserving the charm. Keeping the past alive. The locals considered that property a vital part of the history of the island, but no one had yet gotten around to getting the place registered on the national list for historic preservation." He smirked. "And frankly the place Gloria's father built was— well, *unique* is putting it kindly."

"Is it still there? Do they still use it?"

"Yes, it's there, and no, they put it on the market a year or so ago. I don't think they've been up here since."

"That's so sad."

"Ancient history," Daniel said as he wiped the countertop. "How about you? I mean, are you involved with anyone?"

"Married to my work," Jo said with a laugh. "Like you." But when he didn't seem to buy her banter, she added, "There was one guy back in college. We were together all four years and even attended the same MBA program. Then just went our separate ways."

"Because?"

"We wanted different things from life—he was into making his fortune before he reached thirty. It became something of an obsession."

"And did he succeed?"

Jo blinked as the realization struck her. "I have no idea. We lost touch and I never really kept up with his career—or him." She glanced around the tidy kitchen. "All set here. Thanks for the help."

"Hey, do you want to take a ride? We could drive past the place and you'll see for yourself what had everyone so upset."

Jo hesitated.

"Come on. It's a beautiful night and the fresh air will do us both good."

"Well, you have awoken my curiosity," she admitted.

"Great. I'll run up to the house and let the care worker know how to reach me, and then pick you up. Ten minutes?"

"Sure."

The screen door had not closed all the way before Jo ran to her bedroom. Staring in the mirror, she told herself, *Your hair looks like it got caught in a Weedwacker and, trust me, that lemon-yellow shirt is not your color.*

She changed into a clean white T-shirt, then grabbed a denim jacket from her closet and glanced in the mirror. Better. She ran a brush through her hair and had just finished spitting out mouthwash when she heard his car horn.

This is not a date, she thought as she reached for and then rejected a spritz of cologne.

But when she opened the car door she couldn't help noticing that she wasn't the only one who had freshened up. Daniel was wearing jeans and a white T-shirt that looked like it had come straight off the store shelf. His hair still glistened with droplets of water and he had indeed opted for a splash of aftershave.

Chapter Nine

"It's..."

"A house that belongs maybe in California or Florida, but Nantucket? 'Not so much,' as Jazz would say," Daniel finished as they sat outside the house that Gloria's parents had built. "Gloria herself admits it."

"It's so big. Do they have a large family?"

Daniel laughed. "Just Gloria. That was part of the attraction between us—only children who connected out here on the island."

"So, she came here with her parents for the summer."

"That summer I mentioned—the one I thought would be my last. For Gloria it was her first and last. She was bored silly on the island. My ex—like Jazz—is a city girl through and through."

"Oh, I don't know. Jazz seems to have adapted pretty well, given the fact that she never anticipated she would be spending so much time here. And she's wonderful with Ella."

"Yeah, she is."

Not like Gloria, who finds my mother "quaint." Daniel shook off the thought. He wasn't here to talk about Gloria. He'd suggested this as a way to spend more time with Jo.

Yeah, and what's that about? he wondered.

"I haven't spent much time on this side of the island," she admitted. "It looks like they had magnificent views of the ocean."

"Come on. We'll take a walk." He glanced at her shoes and was relieved to see she was wearing sandals instead of the heels.... Get a hold of yourself before you say or do something foolish, he thought.

He led the way around the side of the dark house to a deck and stairway to the beach. When he reached for her hand to guide her around a cluster of sea oats that had grown up through the slits of the boardwalk, she didn't resist. Then when they reached the relatively level surface of the beach it seemed perfectly natural to just keep holding her hand.

"Jazz seems close to her mother—and to you," Jo said after they'd found the rhythm of walking together and their eyes had adjusted to the pale moonlight.

"Gloria has always treated Jazz more like a younger sister than a daughter. She pretty much leaves the discipline to me, so what's not to like?" Daniel realized he had effectively shut the door on whatever she might have said next in the way of conversation. "Tell me about your mother," he said, and felt her fingers tighten just slightly against his.

"She was amazing. I mean, you being an only child and having only one child, can you imagine what it must have been like for her with seven of us? And she worked full-time."

"How did she die?" Again the slight twitch of her fingers, but he held on and she did not pull her hand away.

"She and Dad were on a sort of second honeymoon last New Year's. They'd gone to a ski resort—a new place that had just opened. Dad had rented the honeymoon suite and there was this balcony. The railing had never been properly attached. She was leaning against it. It gave way. They were on the third floor." Her voice caught.

"I didn't realize it had happened so recently," Daniel said. "I'm really sorry, Jo."

She drew in a shaky breath. "Thanks. You know, the first thing most people say is 'I hope you sued,' as if collecting a boatload of money would make any difference."

"Well, it might have made the resort owners more accountable—I mean, for the future."

"We didn't need to sue. The insurance company paid. Dad gave the money to the seven of us and told us to go do something to make Mom proud. My brother Hank and I used part of it to start this business."

"Why that? Why not give the money to some charity she loved or…"

"Because one thing Mom was really concerned about was the loss of farmland. Farmers getting older and young people not stepping up to take the reins. Hank and I thought if we could somehow help people hang on a little longer, that would make Mom proud."

"I suspect she was very proud of all her children, if you're any example. But is this what you really want to do with your life? What about the dreams and ambitions you had before she died?"

Jo shrugged. "I took life for granted, pretty much. Our family had never truly endured anything close to this before. We were so blessed."

"Yeah, me, too. Growing up here makes the real world seem pretty far away. And then I met Gloria, and six months later we were married and I started working for her father. I thought I had the world by its tail."

"But?"

"But inside there was something else going on. Oh, I

kept telling myself that I should be grateful that I'd been so blessed. That it was selfish to want more."

"Maybe you didn't want more. Maybe you just wanted something different."

He stopped walking and looked down at her, trying to discern her features in the darkness. "That's it," he said. "I never thought of it that way, but that's exactly what I wanted."

She bent down and removed her sandals and shook out some sand, then instead of putting them back on, looped the heel straps over the fingers of her free hand. "You wanted your own hotel," she said as they started walking again. Now she did not dodge the surf that washed up over her feet from time to time.

"Not really. That was more Gloria plus my father-in-law making sure I had a job and could support Jazz."

"So, what did you want?"

It was a simple, direct question. "I didn't know—I still don't."

The conversation should have ended or shifted right there and yet she kept asking the questions that Daniel had not permitted himself to consider. "What got in the way?"

He chuckled. "Life. Mom falling. Jazz buying exam answers. Gloria running off to Paris. And then there's you."

"Me? I have nothing to do with…"

"You've helped me remember where I came from. This island. My family's business. My heritage. And now Jazz's, too." He lifted a shoulder. "Oh, don't get me wrong. The only island that kid wants to live on is Manhattan, but at least now she's beginning to see another side of things."

"So, maybe letting Ella stay on here with help isn't the worst idea?"

Daniel laughed and kicked off his dock shoes as he bent down to roll up the hems of his jeans. "Don't push your luck, lady. I'm thinking about it, okay?"

"It would make a wonderful birthday present."

"I can't give her what's she's already got. And that's enough introspection for one evening." As he stood up he used the palm of his hand to shoot a spray of water at her. He hung around just long enough to hear her sputter a protest before kicking at the surf to splash him, then take off running after him down the beach.

"You do not know who you're messing with, Daniel Armstrong," she shouted.

Daniel slowed down and dodged her efforts to splash water on him until they were both laughing and squealing like children. It felt so good to be this carefree, if only for a moment.

She lunged at him and he caught her easily under her armpits and swung her high off the ground.

"Put me down," she ordered, but she was laughing and her breath came in gasps as she clung to his shoulders.

"Truce?"

"I'm not promising anything."

He scooped her up high in his arms and started walking into the surf.

"Okay, truce," she promised, clinging to his neck, her laughing face only inches from his, and...

He kissed her. The action stunned them both and they hesitated for an instant. Then she kissed him back and this time neither of them pulled away until he had carried her safely back to shore and set her back on firm ground. He pulled away but did not release her as he smoothed back a strand of her short hair that the wind had blown over her eyes.

She was staring up at him, her eyes huge and luminous now in the moonlight and filled with questions. Questions for which he once again had no answers.

* * *

Sleep was not an option. Jo paced the small rooms of the cottage trying to make sense of the evening.

Okay, he kissed you. You kissed him. It was mutual.

"It was the moon and the beach. There cannot possibly be any mutual attraction between you and Daniel Armstrong."

Why not?

Jo ignored her inner voice and continued the conversation with herself aloud. "He is— You have nothing in common."

Except the fact you were both raised on cranberry farms in small New England communities.

"And moved on to totally different lives. It was a freak thing—could have happened to anyone under the circumstances."

She was sure that's the way Daniel was seeing things, if he was thinking about it at all. Once the kiss had ended, he had murmured something about the time and needing to get back and she had rushed in to assure him that she needed to get an early start.

"I found fruitworm eggs in one cranberry bed today," she'd told him as they had walked back to his car, and that change of subject had generated enough questions from him to keep the conversation flowing during the ride home.

"Will you spray?"

"Ella would rather I didn't, but we may not have a choice."

"What, then?"

"There's a product that can be applied through the irrigation system that should take care of the problem. It's expensive but Ella told me to go ahead. 'Nip it in the bud,' were her exact words."

"How does it work?"

Fortunately, her overly detailed explanation of the effectiveness of a biological control agent developed in the lab where she'd worked prevented them from getting personal for the remainder of the ride. At the cottage, she'd practically leapt from the car. "Tell Jazz I'll get to work on those invitation samples tomorrow," she said, and by the time she had completed the sentence she was already at her front door. "See you."

"See you," she mocked herself now. "And then what?" Just how awkward would it be going up to the farmhouse for breakfast and seeing Daniel?

But whatever she might have imagined her next encounter with Daniel might be, she was definitely not prepared for him to greet her with, "Mom's therapist came early, so she'll have to postpone your daily meeting until lunch. Just let me finish up with a couple of calls and then I can help you with the pest treatment. Coffee's still hot and Mom's aide made blueberry muffins."

Jo opened her mouth to say something—anything—but thankfully his cell phone buzzed at the same moment. "I have to take this," he said and flicked the phone on as he moved outside to the porch.

Daniel was still on the phone ten minutes later after Jo had filled one of the travel mugs Ella kept in plentiful supply and headed out to the beds. She couldn't help noticing that his entire demeanor had changed. When he'd taken the call, his voice had been pleasant and all business. But when she passed him, he had one foot up on the porch railing and was running one hand through his hair. He kept saying, "But...but..." while apparently the person on the other end kept talking.

Jo headed off to work, but just when she'd finally managed to put the evening before out of her mind and concentrate on the task at hand, there he was. "Okay, sorry about that. What can I do to help?"

And Jo, feeling peevish that it seemed the kiss had meant nothing to him while she had lost a good night's sleep over it, replied with the first thing that came to mind. "Why would you want to help at all? I mean it would certainly be to your advantage if the crop failed."

She could feel him staring at her in confusion. "What is your problem, lady?"

"You're the one with the problem." She pinched a fruitworm egg and held it up to him. "And if these little buggers have their way, your problems just might be solved."

"Meaning?" he asked tensely.

"Do I really need to spell it out?" she scoffed. "Meaning, this could be your golden opportunity to get Ella to quit farming."

"I really don't need this right now." He growled and stalked back toward the house. Five minutes later Jo heard him rev his car engine, spinning gravel and sand as he took off toward town.

"That went well," she muttered.

The second meeting of the party-planning committee was strained, to say the least. Cyrus had a cold and begged off. Apparently Matt and Jazz had argued about something, since she refused to look his way or acknowledge anything he had to offer. And Daniel sat in a chair close to the door looking as if at any minute he might make a run for it.

Jo sighed. "Hey, people," she said when Jazz and Matt got into a shouting match over whether she would even consider the band Cyrus had suggested. "Hey!"

They all looked at her.

"Let's take a step back here and remember that we are trying to plan a very special day for a very special lady that we all respect and admire."

To her relief, Daniel backed her up. "She's right."

Okay, so he didn't call her by name—just the generic *she*—but it was progress.

"So, maybe we can table the band discussion for now and take a look at the invitations and the guest list. We need to get these out by Monday at the latest so people have a chance to get this on their calendars."

When there were no objections other than Matt checking to see how Jazz was taking this and Jazz's look of indifference, Jo pulled out a folder and laid three different invitations on the kitchen table. She did not miss Jazz's flicker of interest as the teen scooted her chair an inch closer to the table.

"That's cool," Matt ventured, pointing to one sample and looking up at Jazz.

"But look how neat this one is—it folds out into a diamond shape and has the 3-D cranes and the berries," Jazz said, indicating the next sample.

"It'll cost more to mail," Daniel offered, but he took the sample from Jazz and examined it closely, then glanced up at Jo. "It's something different though—and special."

"Like Ella," Jo said.

"Jazz and I could hand-deliver the invitations and then there would be no postage," Matt suggested.

"Plus we'd be sure everyone got theirs and we could make sure they knew to keep it a surprise," Jazz added with a grin at Matt that forgave everything.

"I'll need help making them." Jo waved the guest list. "I mean, all these people?"

"Matt and I will help. You show us how and we can work on them tonight."

"Great idea. I have enough supplies here to get us started and then tomorrow we can pick up the rest."

"Why don't you show the kids how to get started and then you and I can go pick up whatever you need," Daniel offered.

Jo met his look directly for the first time since their argument a few days before, and what she saw there was a challenge. The only question was whether the challenge was coming from him or within herself.

She had to ask herself, Are you ready to be alone with this man without the buffer of work or Ella or these young people?

"Sure," she said with maybe a little too much defiance.

"Fine," Daniel replied, his voice matching hers while Matt and Jazz looked at the two of them as if they would never, ever understand grown-ups. "I'll get the car."

Jo showed Jazz the instructions she'd already written out for all three of the samples, just in case.

"You are so superorganized," Jazz said, and Jo heard it for the compliment it was.

"Okay, so we should be back in an hour, tops," Jo promised, but she might as well have been talking to thin air. Matt and Jazz were already bent over the project, their heads close, their voices a murmur interrupted only by Jazz's giggling.

"Oh, Matt," Jo heard her say.

With Jazz and Matt wrapped up in each other, Jo saw her best chance to avoid spending time with Daniel disappear.

"Shall we go?" Daniel held the door open for her and Jo walked through it.

She could do this. They were just going to the art supply store. No biggie. Really.

Chapter Ten

J̲o had to hand it to Jazz. The girl knew how to put together a party. To everyone's surprise, she selected the church fellowship hall as the site, announcing her decision the next evening as they all gathered to address the invitations.

"But it's perfect," Jazz explained when Jo seemed surprised. "Matt says that Grams is always at the church doing something, so it's the perfect place."

Jo couldn't agree more. After all, everyone knew Ella was a dedicated church member. Until her fall she had always been attending services or choir practice or some special event. More likely, chairing the committee to stage some special event.

When Jo had first realized that Ella was driving to and from the church at night, she'd offered to drive her and gradually had gotten involved herself in some of Ella's committees and campaigns.

"Grams is all excited because the therapist has said she can start going to church again, so Matt and I thought it would be awesome if the party got started right after Sunday services on the weekend of the Fourth."

"Define 'got started,'" Daniel said.

"Well, Dad, we're not going to just do some little church reception and let that be it. This is her seventy-fifth birthday."

Daniel picked up one of the completed handmade invitations and waved it. "Got that part. So there's church and then what?"

"Okay, since everyone gathers in the fellowship hall after services anyway, we're doing a cake and balloons and all that there."

"And then," Matt added, "the plan is to come back here for a picnic in the yard with music and tributes and stuff like that."

"And then that night," Jazz hurried to add, "Mr. Banks and Matt here will drive everyone in wagons out to the beach to watch the fireworks—compliments of the town, of course. It's going to be the *best* party."

"Honey, it all sounds wonderful, but you need to remember that your grandmother is turning seventy-five, plus she's still recovering from major surgery, plus…"

"Dad, we get it. That's why there are these rest periods throughout the day—after the party at the church and then again between the picnic supper and the fireworks. I mean, we need some time in there to change."

"Change what?" Cyrus asked.

"Clothes. We can hardly wear our church clothes for a picnic, and we might need to change again before the fireworks if it's a cool evening, and then there are the costumes."

"Costumes." Daniel said the word as if he'd just recently heard it but wasn't quite sure of the meaning.

"Yes, sir," Matt hurried to explain. "Jazz has this idea about doing a sort of *This Is Your Life* for Mrs. Armstrong where we would play people in her life—at least the ones who have passed on or who can't be here for the party because they live too far away."

"And this little drama is scheduled for—?"

"Right after the picnic and before we leave for the fireworks," Jazz said, consulting a detailed list in the binder she'd put together for managing the party. "I'll play Grams and Matt will play your dad and, Mr. Banks, we thought Matt could also play you as a younger man."

"Long as I don't have to make any speeches," Cyrus grumbled, and Jazz beamed at him.

"So, Matt and I will deliver the invitations tomorrow." She checked her list again. "Dad, could you get the chef at the hotel to suggest a menu and send recipes? And Jo, you did such a wonderful job designing the invitations, maybe you could give some thought to flowers and centerpieces?" Having secured nods of agreement from Jo and her father, Jazz turned to Cyrus. "Oh, and Mr. Banks? That band? Any chance Matt and I could hear them play?"

"Sure thing. They're playing down at the American Legion hall for the folk-dancing tomorrow night. Nine o'clock."

Jazz gave Matt a look that was a pure cry for help.

"It'll be fun," Matt assured her.

"We can all go," Daniel added.

"Count me out," Cyrus protested. "My folk-dancing days are over."

"Jo?"

It's not a date, she reminded herself. It's for the party.

"Sure."

"Great. Then, Matt, you come over around eight-thirty and I'll drive."

"Uh, Dad? No offense, but how about Matt and I meet you and Jo there?"

"Wear a helmet?"

"Aw, Dad. My hair…"

"Your hair will be fine in the car—we'll keep the windows closed, right, Jo?"

Jazz sighed dramatically. "I'll wear a helmet."

* * *

To Daniel's relief, the band was terrific, meeting even Jazz's high standards. Furthermore, his city girl was having the time of her life as she followed the intricate steps of several folk dances with Matt and a group of other young people she seemed to know. Was it possible that his mother was right? Was it possible that he could afford to return to his work and leave her here for the duration of the summer?

His gaze shifted to the back row where Jo had taken her place and was concentrating hard on following the dance steps. So hard that she was biting her tongue and it made her look young and vulnerable. The outfit she'd selected also added to her aura of naiveté and innocence.

She was wearing skinny black jeans and an embroidered peasant blouse with a drawstring neckline and long, full sleeves. Her cap of dark hair shone under the lights and her cheeks were flushed a becoming pink from the effort she was exerting.

She glanced up, caught him watching her and smiled. Then she beckoned for him to join her. He laughed and shook his head. She started toward him and her eyes were sparkling mischievously. She passed Matt and Jazz and nodded toward him and they fell into step with her. Before he knew it he had been corralled onto the dance floor.

He pushed back the sleeves of his sweatshirt, as Jo took both his hands and led him in the steps that Matt and Jazz on either side of them seemed to have learned instantly. To his surprise it was fun. He was having more fun and feeling less stressed than he had in weeks.

The band finished the folk number, then swung immediately into "Goodnight, Irene" as everyone began to leave the dance floor, gathering belongings and heading for the exit. As the last note sounded, everyone still in the building gave the band a prolonged round of applause.

"Well, kid?" The bandleader focused his attention on Jazz. "Cyrus says you're in charge. Are we hired?"

Jazz squinted up at him. "You do that forties big band stuff, right?"

Without missing a beat the leader signaled the others and they launched into an old Glenn Miller standard.

"You're hired!" Jazz proclaimed as soon as they finished. "I'll tell Mr. Banks to get in touch with you with the final arrangements." She offered the man a handshake to seal the deal and in that instant Daniel saw a little more of himself in her. "Okay," she said, turning back to them, "the band's hired, the invites are delivered. We are rocking and rolling here, people."

Outside Daniel and Jo watched to be sure Matt and Jazz donned their helmets before taking off. "Be home by midnight," Jazz called as they sped off.

"Eleven-thirty," Daniel countered, but his voice was lost in the noise of the motor scooter. "As a disciplinarian, I am hopeless," he said as he and Jo started walking to his car.

"Oh, I don't know. *Hopeless* may be going a little too far," Jo countered and then she grinned. "But who am I to contradict you? Hopeless it is."

"Hey, I could use a little support here."

"For your parenting or for your ego?"

"You're a fine one to talk about ego, Miss Cranberry Expert," he said, and they were both laughing now, elbowing each other as they crossed the nearly deserted parking lot.

"I have no ego at all—at least compared to you," she protested, and started to give him a playful punch in the shoulder.

But he caught her hand and she staggered off balance as he reached to steady her by wrapping his free arm around her. And before either of them took the time to recognize the signals they were kissing again.

The one thing I promised myself would not be repeated, he thought. Between his mother, Jazz and work, Daniel had more than enough to deal with. The last thing he needed to throw into this chaotic mess was a romantic entanglement that had little chance of going anywhere. Yet even as the logic of his argument raced through his mind, he moved to deepen the kiss.

She pulled back, but her eyes were still closed and her expression, highlighted by the glow of the streetlamp, was unreadable.

"Jo?"

She opened her eyes. They were dark and bewildered. "I don't get this," she said huskily.

"Neither do I," Daniel admitted. "Got any ideas about what to do about it?"

"We don't even know what 'it' is," she reminded him.

"Right. More than a truce, wouldn't you say?"

She nodded.

"More than—for lack of a better word—animal magnetism?"

"What do you think?" she countered.

"Most definitely more than that," he said as he kissed her lightly on the temple.

"But less than?"

"Impossible? Less than that?" He could practically hear her thinking all the same things he was thinking. Of course, he pondered, the idea of anything developing between us is impossible—at least romantically speaking. I mean, we...

"Well, *impossible* may be going a bit too far." She gazed up at him and grinned. "But then, who am I to contradict someone of your obvious experience?"

She had taken what could have made for an awkward situation for days and turned it into a private joke between them. He'd never known a woman who could defuse a serious and potentially explosive topic the way she could.

"Friends?" he asked as he opened the car door for her.

"For the time being," she said and then laughed. "Now, let's get home so you can be properly installed on Ella's front porch, tapping your foot impatiently when Jazz and Matt come home."

But it wasn't Jazz and Matt that Daniel had to face once they got back to the farm. Jo saw a black town car parked in the drive, motor running while the uniformed driver leaned patiently against the front fender.

"What's happened?" Daniel demanded as both he and Jo practically leapt from the car before it stopped.

"Is it Ella?" Jo added even as she started up the porch steps to the house, where every room seemed to be ablaze with light.

"Daniel," an unfamiliar female voice cried from inside the house.

"Gloria," Daniel acknowledged. "I thought you were in Paris."

"Well, really darling," she replied, stepping out onto the porch. "how could I miss dear Ella's birthday bash?"

"It's supposed to be a surprise," Jo said before she could stop herself.

Daniel's ex-wife flicked her eyes over Jo and dismissed her with a single glance. Instead she fingered the sweat-shirt Daniel was wearing and laughed. "Don't tell me that Ella has managed to turn you back into that raw-edged farm boy I met that summer, Danny."

"Why are you here?" There was no malice or anger in his tone, only weariness.

Gloria came down the steps to where Daniel still waited by the town car. Jo caught a whiff of a perfume that screamed *expensive* and then noticed the deceptively simple but elegant pantsuit, perfectly tailored to Gloria's petite figure. She couldn't help but marvel at the way she balanced effortlessly on the three-inch heels of her peekaboo-toe shoes.

Yep. *Impossible* was the right word, she decided, reflecting on her earlier exchange with Daniel.

"Hey, I'm just going to check on Ella," she said, electing to go inside the farmhouse rather than retrace her steps and have to pass Gloria and Daniel on her way to the cottage.

Gloria spun around and fastened her perfectly made-up dark eyes on her. "Ella is fine, Miss…?"

"It's Jo. Jo Cooper." Jo was pretty sure that a handshake was out of the question. Maybe a curtsy, but definitely not a handshake.

Gloria looked up at Daniel, and Jo saw that she didn't even need to form a question. They'd been married long enough that he knew.

"Ms. Cooper is the woman Ella hired to help her with the cranberry crop this season," Daniel explained.

Gloria waited, her eyes locked on his, a Mona Lisa smile playing over her full lips.

"We—along with Jazz and a friend—went into town to audition a band for Mom's party."

To Jo's complete astonishment, Gloria turned to her with a smile. "Of course. Jasmine has mentioned you and how helpful you've been in planning the party. She told you made the cutest little homemade invitations—perfect for this sort of party."

As she talked, she extended her left hand to Jo. Definitely not a handshake hand, so Jo extended her left hand and before she knew it she was being coaxed down the front stairs, around the town car and onto the path that led her home.

"Jazz said you're taking the cottage for the summer—part of your salary, I believe? We are all so grateful that you were here when Ella took her tumble. Who knows what might have happened?" She shuddered. "You'll be relieved to know that now that our entire family has rallied, you're free to go back to work. You cannot imagine what a comfort it will be to Ella to know that her precious bog is in your capable hands."

Okay, so now the curtsy? Jo thought, impressed in spite of herself with the deft way the woman had taken her out of the picture entirely.

"Nice to meet you, too," she murmured and just kept walking down the path.

"Jo?"

She paused when Daniel spoke her name, realizing he had followed her.

"She's not staying," he said firmly and loud enough for Gloria to hear. "I'll see you tomorrow."

"Mama!" Jazz's surprised shriek penetrated the night as Matt brought his motor scooter to a stop. She flung herself into her mother's arms. "You weren't supposed to be here until day after tomorrow."

"You knew?" Daniel was beginning to look like a runner caught between third base and home plate.

"I got an earlier flight," Gloria explained. "Don't worry, sweetie, your Grams thinks I came because she had the surgery. She has no clue about your fabulous little party." She turned her attention to Matt. "And who is this?"

Matt stepped forward and extended his hand. "Matthew Banks, ma'am. Pleased to meet you."

Gloria pressed Matt's hand with both of hers and hung on. "Oh, Daniel, he is the picture of you that summer. It seems, Matthew, that my daughter and I share a weakness for handsome island boys."

Matt glanced at Jazz as he extricated his hand and climbed onto his scooter. "Like I said, a pleasure, ma'am." He nodded at Jazz and took off.

"Mother!" Jazz protested. "Way to embarrass me big-time."

"What? That? Oh, Jasmine, don't you know by now that the male species loves that sort of thing?"

"Actually, Gloria, speaking for the species, we hate it," Daniel interjected. "It's pretty intimidating to be compared to a girl's father, especially when we're just getting to know the girl. Now, where are you staying?"

Jo took that as her cue to go inside, although she had to admit it was fascinating to watch this little family drama play out. Almost like watching a play onstage. Except this was no play—this was real life.

Fog covered the island for much of the day before Ella's party. Through the open window of her cottage, Jo could hear a discordant choir of voices coming from the farmhouse. Jazz's whine of distress accompanied the steady beat of Gloria's attempts to reassure her daughter. In the days since Gloria's arrival, Jo had learned that Gloria had one surefire solution for any issue—money.

The screen door banged open against the wall of the house and then shut again once Jazz had emerged. Fists clenched, the girl strode down the path on a direct course to the cottage. Jo met her at the door.

"Problems?"

"Ya think? My mother is totally impossible, in case you haven't noticed. She has to take charge of everything. I mean, here we had everything all arranged and she starts changing everything."

Jo held open the door so Jazz could come inside, a move she was sure she would regret. After all, the family dynamics playing out in the farmhouse were hardly her concern.

Jazz folded herself into a chair and stared out the window. "She is flying in some florist—excuse me, *floral designer,* from New York to do the flowers. I tried telling her you had it all under control, but she's decided orchids are perfect for the occasion. Orchids? On a farm? For Grams?"

The girl had a point.

"Well, maybe she just wants to make a contribution to the party," Jo said in a soothing tone.

"No. Nothing I do is ever good enough."

Ah, the crux of the matter, Jo thought.

"I'm sure that's not true, Jazz. What does your dad say?"

"He's up there with her now. I left, but he'll cave. He always does," Jazz pouted.

"Well, you'll know soon enough. He's coming this way—with your mother."

Jazz hunkered down farther into the chair, arms folded protectively around her body as if preparing for battle. Jo went to the door.

"Hi. I'll just go check on something… I'll just go," she finished lamely, trying without success to avoid the daggers emanating directly at her from Gloria's eyes.

"No. Please stay," Daniel coaxed. "Gloria has something to say to both you and Jazz."

"Okay. Jazz is inside."

Daniel held the door for the two women, then followed them into the tiny living room that suddenly seemed more like a closet. Jazz glared at her mother and said nothing. "Shall we all sit down?" Daniel asked.

"I prefer to stand," Gloria murmured, her bright red lips drawn into a tight smile.

"The floor is yours," he said.

"Jasmine," she began, "I had no idea how much this little party meant to you. I…"

"It is not a *little* party," Jazz corrected. "We put together a committee and everything."

"Of course, and you've done a marvelous job here. I was just trying to make a few little suggestions. After all, this is your first attempt and you did call for advice."

Jo found it fascinating the way this woman could take what apparently was supposed to be an apology and twist it to somehow become Jazz's fault.

"Nevertheless…" Daniel prompted.

"Nevertheless, I see now that I was overzealous in my approach and I apologize," Gloria said contritely. "Why don't you come back to town with me so you can explain all the details and we can work on them together over a lovely lunch at the inn?"

Jazz looked directly at her mother for the first time. "The party is tomorrow, Mom. The invitations are out, the replies are in, the food is ordered, the band is hired. There is nothing to work on unless you want to try your hand at baking the birthday cake or guaranteeing fair weather."

"Jasmine, your mother is trying to apologize to you and to Jo here."

Gloria turned slowly to face Jo. "Ah, yes, Josephine, is it?"

"Joanna, but everyone calls me Jo."

Gloria's smile tightened again. "Danny tells me you have been most helpful and Jazz has certainly been singing your praises. You do understand that I had no intention of inserting myself into a…" She glanced quickly at Daniel and then back to Jo. "A *developing situation.*"

Jo had her own arsenal of tight smiles and pulled one out now. "Define 'developing situation.'"

Daniel buried his face in his hands and Jazz uncurled herself and sat forward as if ready to observe a catfight.

"A turn of phrase," Gloria said. "I'm sure your little country bouquets will be just fine. Charming, even. Yes, I can see now that they set a certain tone." She turned to Daniel, meaning she turned her back to Jo. "Shall we get back? Ella will be finished with her therapy. Perhaps we could *all* go into town for a lovely family lunch at the inn—my treat."

Ignoring the lunch invitation, Daniel stood and looked at Jazz. "You okay?"

His daughter nodded.

"Need me to help with anything for the party today?" he asked.

"Matt said he'd have a bunch of kids at the church by ten to decorate the fellowship hall, and we still have to paint the plywood tabletops his grandfather cut for us and…"

"I can do that," Jo volunteered. "I'll call Cyrus and have him bring the boards to the machine shed. We can open both ends and have plenty of ventilation, plus it's out of sight of the house."

"Well, I can certainly manage a paintbrush," Gloria said. "I'll just need a ride to town, Daniel, so I can change into something more appropriate."

To everyone's surprise Daniel burst out laughing. Then Jazz did as well.

"What?" Gloria demanded.

"Come on, Mom, the idea you have anything remotely close to appropriate for painting plywood tabletops boggles the mind."

"I have jeans and T-shirts," she huffed as she headed out to the car.

And indeed she did. Jo and Cyrus had just finished unloading the last of the diamond-shaped boards and lining them up along the walls of the shed when Cyrus spotted Gloria coming their way.

"What on earth?" he muttered.

Gloria was wearing tight, black designer jeans that looked as if they'd come straight off the showroom floor, a hot-pink, fitted knit top that by any stretch of the imagination could not be called a T-shirt, and a flowing print scarf knotted around her throat. Her boots reminded Jo of the expensive pair Jazz had nearly ruined in the bog. She was balancing a cardboard tray.

"I thought perhaps a latte might energize the workers," she said.

Jo accepted the gesture for the peace offering she assumed it to be. "Perfect," she said, relieving Gloria of the tray and distributing the coffee. "Cyrus?"

Cyrus accepted the cup and pulled off the cover. "I don't usually drink this fancy stuff," he told Gloria. "Ella likes her coffee black and strong and so do I, but there's a first time for everything." He took a long swallow. "Sweet," he managed to gasp out.

"Black and strong," Gloria said. "Next time I'll remember that. How's yours?"

Jo sipped at the frothy liquid. "Fine. Good. Thanks."

Gloria beamed as she took a sip of her own latte and turned her attention to the boards. "My, you're so organized."

Cyrus saw that as his cue to explain the process to her. Each board was to be painted forest green, cranberry red or white. He opened paint cans and displayed the range of colors.

"One tiny suggestion," Gloria said, her smile now trained on Cyrus. "If we mix just the tiniest bit of the red or green into the white, it will soften the color ever so slightly."

"I think Jazz would be fine with that," Daniel said, stepping inside the shed.

Jo noticed that he was wearing a pair of well-worn jeans and a paint-spattered T-shirt that looked as if it had been around for decades. Suddenly she felt better about her own cutoff coveralls over a cotton tank.

While Gloria directed the mixing of the paint, Daniel helped Jo move the first of the boards onto the workhorses. "How about Jo and I get started on the green and cranberry boards and you two handle the white?" he called over his shoulder.

"Works for me," Cyrus agreed with a grin at Gloria.

"Yes. Lovely," Gloria replied, and Jo couldn't help noticing that the tight smile was back.

Chapter Eleven

Ella was beaming as she walked down the aisle of the church on the arm of her only son, using the cane Cyrus had carved and presented to her that morning. And everyone already seated in the pews on either side smiled, reached forward to touch her or waved their welcome.

Heartened by such a display of love and respect for his mother, Daniel remembered something Ella had once told him. "If you can find your place in the world—a place where your being there makes a real difference to those around you—then you have found wealth beyond imagination." Ella Armstrong had clearly found that place. Daniel couldn't help wondering if he would ever be so blessed.

At Ella's insistence Jo had agreed to sit with the family. So as Ella and Daniel walked down the center aisle followed by Gloria and Jazz, he saw Jo slip down the side aisle and take her place on the far end of the pew. He waited for Jazz and then Gloria to slide in, then saw Matt and Cyrus enter the church and beckoned them forward.

Jazz quickly made a place for Matt next to her, and Daniel indicated Cyrus should take the aisle next to Ella. As the organist sounded the last chords of the prelude,

Daniel hurried back up the aisle and down the side to slide in next to Jo.

"We should switch," she whispered, indicating that his place should be next to Gloria. The minister called for all to stand and join in the responsive reading and remain standing for the first hymn.

"This is fine," Daniel told her, then opened the hymnal to the selected reading and passed the hymnal to Gloria. Then he opened a second and held it so that Jo was sharing at the same time that Gloria thrust her hymnal Jo's way. "Got it covered," Daniel whispered to Gloria with a smile.

Ella cleared her throat and gave her son a look of warning. He grinned sheepishly and turned his attention to the words on the page.

He couldn't help noticing that, while most of the congregation read the words in a kind of rote monotone, Jo gave the words expression and emphasis as if she were really seeing them and taking them to heart. Her enthusiasm for the reading and then the old, familiar hymn reminded him that there had been a time when his faith had been the very foundation of his life. The years he had attended this church with his parents and grandparents. When he had led the youth group and participated in missions to help rebuild houses destroyed by fire or flood. When he and his friends had gone to West Virginia and worked for a summer to organize a food bank and tutoring for disadvantaged children. When his life had meant something and made a difference.

In the close quarters of the pew he could feel Jo's shoulder pressed against his, could smell Gloria's signature perfume. He glanced down and saw that both women had their hands folded in their laps. Gloria's manicured and painted nails contrasting with Jo's unadorned fingertips. Gloria's multiple diamond rings catching the light of the sun. Jo's single thin, silver band with a patina that spoke of treasured memories. A friendship ring? A token of a lost love?

Lost love? Daniel realized he had no idea if she was involved with someone or not. They had kissed—twice. Surely she would have said something. But he hadn't asked. What did he know about her, really? What did he want to know about her?

He forced his thoughts away from Jo and looked down the row to where his mother sat, as tall and straight as she had when he was a boy. But she looked older and more frail and Daniel regretted that sooner rather than later things would have to change for her.

The minister called for a moment of silent meditation before the closing prayer, and every head bowed. And Daniel Armstrong was struck by another memory—a memory of a time when he would turn to God anytime he was unsure or confused about the path he was about to take. To his surprise the words came as easily as if he had been praying every day of his life.

Father, thank You for this day and for what it is going to mean to my mother. She has spent a lifetime caring for and giving to others. Let this day that my daughter has planned for her be as perfect as Jazz imagines. Thank You for my daughter—for this child who surprises me every day and reminds me of my true purpose here on this earth. And as we go forward together, please show me the right path to take with both my mother and my child. And finally, thank You for Jo and what she has meant to my mother and to Jazz—and to me. Even if it be Your will that she is only a temporary buffer in the storms we've been chosen to face at this time, may she find from us what we have found with her—kindness, companionship and...

His thoughts trailed off as the minister launched into his own closing prayer. *And what?*

The organist struck up the postlude and everyone headed up the aisles and downstairs to the fellowship hall. Daniel noticed that several neighbors stopped to speak to Ella, deliberately delaying her until everyone could get in place for the surprise awaiting her. Jo and Jazz had already slipped out of the pew and disappeared.

As planned, after the reception they returned to Star Pond and Ella went to lie down for a nap, unaware of the surprises Jazz had in store for her. As Jazz flitted around making sure everything was perfect for the buffet, Jo couldn't help thinking how different the girl was from the angry, sullen teen who had arrived on the island just six weeks earlier. Daniel had been right to bring her here. Perhaps he was right about Ella as well. For as hard as Ella had worked on her therapy, there was no question that she was slower and less sure of herself than she'd been before her fall.

Still, she was in her glory here on this small island she had called home her entire life. Everyone—young, old and in between—seemed to know her. Not only know her but have some attachment to her. Jo couldn't help thinking of her own mother and the way she'd touched the lives of so many. It was one reason Jo and her brother Hank had decided to start the temp business for area farmers. "Mom would be all over this idea," Hank had said, and Jo couldn't argue. So she had left her corporate job along with its benefits and bonuses and poured all of her savings, along with the insurance from her mother's accident, into this business.

But she had failed to consider the single downside of her decision—that she would become attached to the people she served and then have to leave.

"Hi." Daniel flopped into the lawn chair next to hers and handed her a bottle of cold water. "Quite a party."

"Thanks for the water," she said as she twisted the cap off and took a swallow.

"Speaking of the party…Jazz couldn't have pulled this off without you, Jo. She knows it and so do I." He pointed to Ella where she sat in the middle of a swarm of neighbors and friends. She was laughing and gesturing excitedly, obviously in the middle of some story. "Look at her," Daniel said. "She's having the time of her life."

"She sure is," Jo agreed. "Does she know about the hayride?"

"Nope. Jazz's party philosophy seems to be one of 'keep the surprises coming.' She's been pretty wired about this whole thing. I'm glad it's all going so well."

"She's a good kid."

Daniel chuckled. "That wasn't what you were thinking the first time you two met."

"Well, no, not exactly. But we're all guilty of stereotyping from time to time."

"What did you think of me?"

Jo was surprised at the question. *Why do you care?* she wondered.

"Come on, Jo. A little truth or dare? Tell me the truth or accept a dare?"

"What's the dare?"

"Not telling until you choose."

"What are you—eight?" Jo laughed and bought time by drinking the rest of her water. "Okay. When I first saw you at the hospital, I thought you didn't match up to what Ella had told me about you."

"How so?"

"You're sure you want to know this?"

"I can take it."

"Ella described a man firmly in charge of things. A man who could take any negative situation and turn it into a positive." Jo squirmed sideways in her chair so she was facing him. "She once told me about a time when you were maybe sixteen and an early frost was coming and the sprinklers weren't in yet and…"

"I called all my friends and told them to raid their mothers' linen closets. So we went out and covered all the vines with sheets and tablecloths and anything else we could scrounge up," he recalled. "How could I have forgotten that? It was an incredible feeling to see the way my dad looked at me that night. We'd had this ongoing fight about my wanting to leave the island, and that night I realized that I might not have his blessing but I had his respect. I had thought he didn't believe I could handle life off the island, but that night I realized that he couldn't handle my leaving."

"What happened?"

"I stayed. Through college and grad school, including the winter he had a heart attack and died. It was Mom who urged me to leave after that. I had met Gloria that summer and we were getting pretty serious, but when Dad died I had every intention of coming back here."

"But you didn't."

"No." He shook off the memory. "So, you told me what you expected, but what did you think?"

Jo stood up. "Putting it in the kindest possible terms, I thought you were a man who ran his life like a business and when people didn't play by those rules, you had trouble adjusting."

Daniel looked up at her, squinting against the setting sun. "And now?"

"One truth per customer."

When the hay wagons arrived, Daniel and Matt lifted Ella onto the seat of the wagon Cyrus was driving while

Jazz scrambled to take a similar spot on the wagon Matt would drive. Guests clambered aboard, their excitement evident in their loud chatter and laughter. Jo lifted the last toddler up to his mother's arms and then stepped back.

"Come on," Daniel called, extending a hand to help her aboard.

"I'm staying here to get everything cleared away."

"We can do that in the morning. Come on."

"Now, Danny, leave the woman alone. She's earned a little peace and quiet. After all she's done today." Gloria smiled benevolently at Jo.

"I guess we could wait until morning," Jo said. "Let me just put the food away and I'll meet you out there."

"You see, Danny. She has everything under control."

To the surprise of both women, Daniel jumped down from the wagon. "I'll give you a hand. Then we can both follow in the truck." He signaled to Cyrus to move out. "Jo and I will be there before the first firecracker," he promised.

Jo had already started to carry platters of food back inside. "There's not that much," she said when Daniel followed, balancing the second birthday cake of the day. "We got everything that needed refrigeration put away earlier on."

"I stayed for another reason," he said, and his tone was so serious that Jo was almost afraid to look at him.

"Because?"

She heard him set the cake on the table and then felt his hands on her shoulders. He turned her so that she was facing him and lifted her chin with his forefinger. "Because I wanted to thank you. I can't remember a day when my mother has been the center of attention and loving it. Usually she's the one serving everyone else, but today she was happier than I've seen her since before Dad died."

"She has so many people who love her, and she's unique in that she realizes her blessings. She once told me that she starts and ends every day counting those blessings and adding new ones."

"Like you."

Jo shrugged. "I'd say I got the best of this deal."

"Maybe, but you've not only been there for my mother, you've made an enormous difference in Jazz's settling in here this summer."

"I'd have to say Matt is the one who made that work," Jo said with a laugh. "Never underestimate the power of a handsome and caring young man to impress a girl like Jazz."

"And what kind of man impresses you, Jo Cooper?"

She pulled away and busied herself covering the food. "We're not talking about me."

"I am." Daniel reached for the glass dome his mom had used to cover her cakes for as long as he could remember. "I'm actually asking you if maybe we might think about seeing each other—getting to know each other a little better. I mean, once things here are under control. Would you ever consider coming to New York for a few days?"

"I might. Of course, I'd have to think about where to stay," she added, and purposely made her tone light and teasing.

"Hey, you're in luck. I happen to know the owner of this really cool hotel right in the heart of the city."

"That might work."

"We could see a couple of Broadway shows," he said. "If you like that sort of thing and, judging by the CDs I saw in the cottage, you do."

"I'm not a total hick, Daniel Armstrong. I have seen plays on Broadway before and, yes, I've been to the top of the Empire State Building, seen the Statue of Liberty and toured Ellis Island."

They were working in easy rhythm now, both as familiar with Ella's kitchen as if they'd lived here for years.

"Guess I'll have to come up with new adventures, then. Fortunately, the city offers an endless array of things to see and do." He wiped the counter and folded the dish towel. "So you'll come?"

"After the harvest," she agreed. "Now come on or we'll miss the fireworks." She pulled off her apron and hung it on a hook by the back door, then switched off the light. "Lock up," she reminded him as she started across the yard toward her truck.

She heard the lock click and then he caught up with her and pulled her into his arms. "Thanks again for everything," he murmured as he lowered his lips to hers.

And as they kissed, Jo was vaguely aware of the sky turning red, blue and golden as the first of the fireworks exploded.

From the moment they arrived to see the remainder of the fireworks, Daniel had hold of Jo's hand. All day long he had watched her, thought about the way she moved so easily among people he'd known his entire life who she had known for only a matter of weeks. He watched her with his mother, the two of them laughing together like sisters. He saw the way Jazz would turn to her for reassurance that everything indeed was going as planned.

When he'd stayed behind to help clean up after the picnic, he'd thought only to have a private moment to let her know how genuinely grateful he was. He'd wanted to make sure she understood, no matter how things turned out, that he respected her work and was grateful for what she had done for his mother and daughter.

And for me, he thought.

He wrapped his arm around her shoulders and pulled her

close, as the skies lit up with a kaleidoscope of green and gold and red and blue, and the glowing remains floated into the bay. Cyrus had one arm casually resting across the back of Ella's chair, and Jazz was leaning on Matt's shoulder.

But then Cyrus was standing, glancing around as he bent over Ella, and shouting something that was lost in the noise of the grand finale.

"Something's wrong," Daniel said and pulled Jo along with him as he made his way through the crowd to reach his mother. Ella seemed disoriented, her eyes glassy while beads of sweat dotted her forehead.

"She was fine," Cyrus said, his voice shaking. "Just a minute ago she said she'd never forget this day."

Daniel handed his cell to Jo. "Call 911, now." He bent next to Ella's chair and took her hand. "Mom?"

To his relief she stirred and opened her eyes a slit. "It hurts," she said and when she closed her eyes her lashes were wet.

"Where?"

"My head, and I can't feel my fingers or toes on this side and…"

"Paramedics are on their way," Jo assured him. "What can I do?"

The last firecracker had sounded and people were beginning to realize something had happened to Ella.

"Doc," Cyrus shouted and a man turned and hurried over.

"What happened?" he asked as he took Ella's pulse and made a cursory examination.

Cyrus filled him in.

"Mrs. Armstrong," the doctor said loudly as the sirens of an ambulance pierced the sudden silence. "Can you open your eyes?"

"Rather not," Ella said, and her words were slurred.

"Get those people out of the way so the paramedics can pull in close," he ordered.

But there was little need for instructions. These were island people and they had already assessed the situation and understood their role in it was to stay out of the way.

"Grams?" Jazz fought her way through the circle of friends and ran to Ella. "Daddy?"

"The doctor's here, honey. Let's let him and the paramedics do their jobs, okay?"

"But she'll be okay, right?" She glanced wildly around the circle, looking for reassurance, and spotted Gloria, cell phone to ear.

"I don't care about the cost, Daddy," Gloria implored. "This is Daniel's mother—Jasmine's grandmother. We need an immediate medical evacuation tonight."

Gloria anxiously made arrangements with her father while the paramedics got Ella onto a gurney, hooked up to oxygen and into the ambulance with the doctor. A few minutes later she clicked off the phone and embraced Jazz, who was sobbing now.

"It's my fault," she blubbered. "It was too much. We should have…"

"No place for 'should haves,' Jazz, honey. Let's not panic. We'll go to the hospital. Meanwhile Papa Barrington will take care of everything. You'll see."

Daniel realized she was using the name Jazz had given his father-in-law, and it had a calming effect on their daughter. He met Gloria's eyes, meaning to show gratitude, but instead was stunned to realize that she was every bit as distraught as he was.

"Can we use the truck?" he asked Jo.

"Of course." She pulled the keys from her pocket and prepared to toss them to him.

"You drive. I need to… I…"

Jo was next to him in an instant. "Go to them," she said as she touched his face. "I'll get the truck."

Daniel nodded. When he looked up, Gloria was once again on her phone and Jazz was hanging on to her as if she were a lifeline.

Chapter Twelve

Once the emergency team at the Nantucket hospital had run several tests and made a preliminary diagnosis of stroke, everyone agreed that Ella should be transferred to a special stroke treatment center in Manhattan. Through hand gestures and garbled, slurred speech Ella insisted that Jo come with them. As soon as arrangements were made to transport Ella in a medical evacuation helicopter, Daniel, Gloria, Jazz and Jo headed for the airport to board the private jet that Gloria's father had sent.

Jo could not help but be impressed at the power of money to make seemingly impossible things happen. The minute they touched down in New York, a car was waiting on the tarmac to take them to the stroke center. By the time they arrived, Ella had been admitted and was resting comfortably in a private room that looked more like a luxury hotel suite than a hospital room. From the moment they'd all boarded the private jet, Jo had tried to make herself as inconspicuous as possible. She shouldn't have worried. Daniel and Gloria had focused all of their attention on Jazz, who was inconsolable, insisting that she had caused Ella's stroke.

"It was too much," she whispered over and over again, heedless of her parents' assurances that the events of the day had had nothing to do with Ella's stroke.

In the town car, Jo rode up front with the driver, leaving the backseat for the family. *The family.* For surely that's what they were. And who was she in all of this? She couldn't help thinking as she sat in the small sitting area outside Ella's hospital room. The hired hand? Ella's friend? Daniel's…

"You okay?" Daniel asked as he collapsed onto the couch next to her.

"Fine," she replied. "How's Ella?"

Daniel smiled wearily. "Still trying to give orders."

"That's a good sign, then."

"She's asking for you. Why don't you go in for a minute? I need to call Cyrus and let him know she's stable and settled." He pulled out his cell and punched in the number, then paced the room and out into the hall as he waited for the call to go through.

Jo heard Gloria quietly reassuring Jazz as the two of them left Ella's room and headed down the hall. Her voice was a mother's lullaby, and Jo could not help recalling her own mother's calm, comforting words in the midst of any tragedy, large or small. Her heart broke for Jazz, and she was glad that Gloria had decided to come to Nantucket.

"Jo!"

Ella's sounding of her name was as sharp and clear as ever, and Jo smiled as she moved to Ella's bedside and took her hand. "Right here," she assured her.

But when Ella turned to look at her, Jo saw the fear in the older woman's eyes, saw the tear that leaked from one bright eye, saw the mouth twisted by paralysis the doctors had assured them might be temporary. And most of all, she felt the unresponsive hand—the fingers curled into a fist, unyielding even as Jo stroked the knuckles with her thumb.

"It's going to be all right," Jo said softly, parroting the platitudes that came so easily at times like this, when a person was not at all sure things would ever be the same again.

Ella's good hand flailed helplessly. Her lips moved as she tried to form the words that refused to come. Finally, she closed her eyes tight and with sheer force of will blurted out, "Stay."

"I'm not going anywhere," Jo assured her.

Ella's face contorted once again as she rocked her head fiercely from side to side.

"Stay? Stay where?" Jo tried hard to interpret what Ella so desperately needed to tell her. "Nantucket?"

Ella stilled and Jo gently smoothed back a strand of gray hair. "Of course. Don't worry, Ella. I'll go back to Nantucket tomorrow. I'll…"

Again the flailing hand, the rocking back and forth, the twisted mouth spitting out a garbled protest. "Me!"

Jo had never felt so helpless. "I don't understand," she murmured as she turned Ella's outburst of seemingly unrelated words over and over in her mind.

Help me, Father. I want her to know I understand.

Jo leaned closer to Ella, who had slumped back onto the pillows, exhausted and defeated. "Are you trying to tell me you want to stay on Nantucket?"

The working side of Ella's mouth turned up slightly and her breathing eased. And as if someone had entered the room and flicked on the overhead light, Jo got it.

"Now you listen to me, Ella Armstrong. We need to strike a bargain here. You promise me that you will do everything possible to get yourself well, and I promise you I will champion your cause to return to Nantucket. Deal?"

Jo thrust out her hand and Ella grasped it firmly with

her good hand and shook it. Then with surprising strength she hung on and pulled Jo closer. Apparently, she had something else she wanted Jo to handle.

"Thaniel." She struggled to find the right syllables.

"Daniel went to call Cyrus. He'll be right back," Jo told her. "Now, that's enough for tonight. You need your rest, and frankly I'm exhausted and need to find a hotel room. I'll stop by in the morning, okay?"

Ella closed her eyes and her grip went slack. Jo kissed her forehead and turned to tiptoe out of the room. Daniel was standing in the doorway, and Jo realized that when Ella had called his name it was because he'd been standing there.

"How's Jazz?" she asked as she stepped past him to get her purse.

"A little calmer. Gloria took her home." He glanced around the room as if checking to be sure they hadn't forgotten anything. "Ready to go? The staff assures me they'll call if there's any change, and I could use a shower."

"You go on, then. I'll be fine." Jo started down the hall toward the elevator.

"You're not heading back to Nantucket tonight, are you?"

"Of course not. I'll get a hotel room and…"

Daniel arched one eyebrow. "I happen to own a hotel, and as I said, it's two blocks from here."

"But…"

"Please tell me you aren't going to debate this. Frankly, it's been a day, and I'm so beat I don't think I could hold up my end of things."

Jo smiled as the elevator arrived and they stepped inside. "I just thought you might be fully booked and didn't want to impose."

"Impose already," he said as he wrapped his arm around her shoulders. "Gives me a sense of being in some control in a world that seems to be imploding all around me."

* * *

On the walk to the hotel, they talked about Ella and the doctor's prognosis for her recovery, but skirted any discussion of what that might mean for Ella's future.

"Here we are," Daniel announced as they approached the corner. "Home sweet home." He stood aside, allowing her to enter one section of the revolving door and then following in the next.

The lobby of the Barrington Hotel had a charming 1930s ambience that made Jo feel as if the revolving door had in fact been some kind of time machine. "It's lovely," she said as she glanced around.

In spite of the hour, the lobby was filled with clusters of guests and the feeling of a lovely party. People chatted and laughed and called out to one another from across the room. And Daniel moved through the gathering like a good host, greeting people, asking if they were enjoying their stay, pausing to hear of a man's concern with the location of his room and then signaling a staff member to come and take care of the problem.

She couldn't help noticing that he greeted his staff by name and that they seemed genuinely happy to see him at this unexpected hour. To her surprise the elevators were staffed by a uniformed employee who smiled broadly when he saw Daniel.

"Busy night, boss," the elderly man said as he slid the polished-brass gate closed and pressed a button for the ride up.

"Gus, this is Jo Cooper, a friend of my mother's."

"Nantucket?" Gus asked.

"For the summer," Jo replied as she accepted the man's handshake.

"Gus has been the night-shift elevator operator for— what is it now, Gus?"

"Stopped counting at thirty-nine years," Gus replied, and then winked at Jo. "Also stopped counting my age at thirty-nine."

"Ms. Cooper will be staying in the penthouse for a few days while my mother is here in the hospital."

"Nothing serious, I hope?"

"A mild stroke, according to the doctors. We're hoping for a full recovery," Daniel assured him, but Jo saw that his optimism was purely for the benefit of his employee.

"I'll keep her in my prayers, boss," Gus said as they reached the top floor and he held the door open for them. "Nice to meet you, Ms. Cooper."

"It's Jo, please, and it was my pleasure."

Gus grinned and let the door slide shut as Jo turned to find herself in a small, sterile apartment. "This is lovely, but a single room would have sufficed."

"I want you to be comfortable." Daniel moved around the apartment, opening the doors to the terrace, checking the bathroom and kitchen. "I'll have room service bring up some fruit and breakfast items. Coffee, juice…"

"Daniel, I can eat in the coffee shop downstairs or at the hospital. There's really no need to…"

But he was already on the phone. Again Jo noticed that he called the person in room service by name, asked after the woman's child and then made his order. Her respect for the gracious way he treated his employees kicked up a notch. If the temp farmer business ever reached the point where she and Hank needed to hire additional help, she would remember to follow Daniel's example.

"Okay, so that's set," Daniel announced. "I also asked them to stop by the gift shop and bring you up some toiletries and one of our souvenir nightshirts. Tomorrow we'll go shopping."

"I have clothes, Daniel," she said, assuming he meant her clothes were not exactly appropriate for city wear.

"Yeah, I know, but they're in a closet on Nantucket and you're here—at least for a few days."

"You've got a point. I'll pick up a couple of things in the morning."

The elevator groaned into action and a moment later a staffer arrived pushing a teacart filled with supplies.

"Daniel Armstrong," he said as he greeted the young woman. "You're new?"

Very new and very unused to meeting the boss, judging by the expression on the woman's face, Jo observed.

"Aretha Taylor," the woman murmured with a shy smile.

"Well, Aretha, this is Ms. Cooper and if she calls, be sure she gets whatever she needs, okay?"

"Yes, sir," Aretha replied, her voice more assured now that she was back on the more familiar ground of employer/employee.

Once everything had been stored in its place, Daniel rang for the elevator. When it arrived, Aretha boarded with the empty cart and Gus held the door for Daniel.

"Call the desk if you need anything, and you have my cell," he told Jo. "I'll let you know if there are any changes."

Jo realized she was on the verge of bursting into tears as the events of the last several hours finally sank in. Unable to manage words, she nodded.

Daniel lifted her chin with his forefinger and kissed her forehead. "It's all going to work out," he said softly. "Get some rest."

Jo nodded. "Call if there's any change," she reminded him as he stepped into the elevator.

"Get some sleep," he replied and, as the elevator doors slid shut, Jo could hear him chatting with Gus and Aretha, gathering details about his new employee that he would no doubt file away for their next encounter.

The noise of the city along with Jo's concern for Ella kept her up most of the night. She paced the apartment, finding little comfort in the sterile surroundings. Finally she settled into a chaise on the terrace and watched daylight come over her limited view of Central Park. At least it was green in the landscape of concrete, steel and glass that surrounded her on all other sides.

But the sight of the park brought her right back to her concern for Ella. A fractured hip was one thing, but a debilitating stroke? How would she manage?

You promised, Jo reminded herself.

But what if Daniel had been right all along? What if the best place for Ella was here, where her family could care for her?

Nantucket is where she wants to be, Jo's inner voice said.

"I don't know what to do, dear Father. How can I go back on my word? And yet, surely Ella was just frightened by all that's happened and clinging to some modicum of control when her world was spiraling out of control. Surely once she has time to accept the frailty of her health, she'll recognize that she needs to be closer to family."

Jo closed her eyes and tried to imagine Ella here in the city. Oh, she would do fine, but would she be happy?

"This is the day the Lord hath made," she had announced the first morning Jo had gone to share breakfast with her. The rain had been falling in sheets as thick as Ella's pea soup and the day promised no letup from the damp chill that permeated everything. But Ella had grinned at Jo and added, "Let us be glad and rejoice in it."

And that had been the pattern through all the weeks they

had worked together. Ella found pure delight in every facet of the island—the unpredictable weather, the quirky residents, the inconvenience and expense of island living. But most of all she found peace and contentment in her cranberry farm, grieving momentarily over the loss of acreage over the years, but determined to hang on to what was left. To offer it as her legacy to her only child and her only grandchild. "Whether they appreciate the place now or not," she'd told Jo.

No, a promise was a promise. If Ella wanted to live out her days on the land she had tended for all of her adult life, then so be it.

Jo stood at the terrace railing, found a patch of sky and whispered, "Thank You, God, for showing me the way. Please hold Ella in Your care and help me know how best to help her achieve her heart's desire to return home as soon as possible."

The jangle of the phone startled her, but because she was feeling more positive than she had since Ella's collapse, Jo grinned as she ran to pick it up. "Good morning."

Daniel chuckled. "And good morning to you. I thought maybe I was calling too early."

"I'm a farm girl, remember? Up with the rooster's crow— or in this case the crash of the trash bin. How's Ella?"

"According to the nurse, she had a good night. Of course, I imagine the medication helped. I'm headed over there now so I don't miss the doctor's visit. Want to come?"

"If you think it would be all right."

"Jo, Mom thinks of you as family." A beat and then, "And so do I. I'll see you in the lobby in ten minutes?"

"Fifteen," Jo bargained.

"Sheesh, I thought you farm girls were up and raring to go at the first crash of a Dumpster," he teased.

"Cute. Fifteen minutes," she said, and hung up.

* * *

The news was better than Daniel had expected, and yet the doctor's prognosis fell significantly short of promising a full recovery.

"What's your best guess?" Daniel asked.

"Given Mrs. Armstrong's age and state of health prior to the stroke, I would expect that she will respond well to therapy. Her speech has already begun to clear and she might even regain limited use of the affected extremities. The fact that she has some movement in her fingers and toes is a positive sign. But the road ahead of her is a grueling one. Many patients become discouraged by the slowness of any real progress and give up."

The very idea that his mother might ever give up on anything was laughable. But when the doctor suggested Daniel and Jo tour the rehabilitation facilities of the stroke center, Daniel experienced his first real doubts that Ella might ever regain the strength she would need to live independently again.

"Daniel?" Jo took his arm and led him to a bench. "Come sit down. You're white as a sheet."

"I'm okay," he protested, but he sat down, buried his face in his hands and let the tears come. "She's always been the rock."

"She still is," Jo assured him as she squeezed his hand. "Don't sell Ella short, Daniel. She'll do whatever it takes. She's that determined to get back to Nantucket."

Daniel's head shot up and he swiped away the remnants of his tears with one fist. "She can't go back there, Jo. You heard the doctor. Best case scenario, she won't be confined to a wheelchair."

"That's the doctor. He doesn't know Ella."

"Look at them," Daniel whispered, indicating patients struggling to take even one tiny step. They clung to the parallel bars of the walkway even as a therapist hung on to a belt strapped to the patient's waist and an aide followed closely with a wheelchair.

"Yes. They are struggling," Jo agreed, "but look at their faces when they achieve even the smallest victory."

The man on the parallel bars slung one limp foot forward, then stepped forward again with his good leg. Both he and the therapist were beaming as the man collapsed into a wheelchair, exhausted but triumphant.

"But…"

"Do not give up on Ella before you even give her the chance to try," Jo said. "Now, let's get back to her room so you're there when she gets back from her MRI."

When they reached Ella's room, Gloria was there bustling about, unpacking several shopping bags and storing the contents in the dresser drawers and closets.

"Necessities," she announced when she saw Daniel. "How they expect a woman to make any attempt at recovery dressed in those horrific hospital gowns is beyond me." She held a print silk robe with satin collar up to herself and arched an eyebrow. "I had to guess at the size but I think this will do."

"Mom will love it," Daniel said, indicating that Jo should take the single chair while he stood by the window. "How did you manage all of this with the shops not yet open?"

"I called Raul and he insisted on meeting me first thing so I could choose a few things."

"Is Jazz with you?"

"No, I left her to sleep. Poor darling was exhausted and beyond terrified when we left here last night." She turned her attention briefly to Jo and then continued unpacking toiletries and setting them out on the dresser top. "Perhaps the party was not the best idea. The stress and excitement could have…"

"Do not say anything approaching that in front of Jazz,"

Daniel ordered. "She's already blaming herself. The party was delightful—a perfect way to celebrate Mom's diamond year. The doctor says the stroke would have happened with or without the party."

Gloria shrugged. "Well, whatever the cause, that's the past. The future is that we must make sure that dear Ella has the very best of care."

"I'm already looking into that. I have appointments with the social worker, the rehab team and the doctors here at the stroke center scheduled for this afternoon. The social worker can provide a list of facilities for us to tour."

"Ella wants to go home," Jo said.

"Ella is in no position to know what she wants, poor dear," Gloria retorted.

"She's had a stroke. She's not senile or demented." Jo's voice had that tight, controlled timbre that Daniel had come to recognize as a sign she was losing patience fast.

"Ladies, please. It's premature to even think about where Mom might end up. I'm just gathering information at this point. She'll be here for at least another couple of weeks—perhaps as long as a month."

"Of course, you're right, Danny," Gloria crooned as she edged closer to Daniel and turned her back on Jo. "Perhaps given the circumstances," she murmured, "Ella's visitors should be limited to family for the time being?"

"Jo is family," Daniel replied, but Jo had already started for the door. "Jo?"

"I need to do a little shopping," she said, her smile bright but wavering. "Tell Ella I'll stop by later."

She was halfway to the elevator before he caught up with her. "Don't mind Gloria, She's just—well, Gloria."

"And yet she has a point," Jo said. "Right now Ella needs her family around her and that doesn't include me. Don't worry. I'll be back."

"Promise? 'Cause truth is—we need to talk about this business of Mom returning to Nantucket. We both know that's impossible and we need to present a united front, Jo."

The elevator doors opened and several people inside pressed back to make room for Jo. "Not going to happen," she called as the doors slid shut.

Chapter Thirteen

Jo spent most of the next week at the stroke center. Daniel juggled his work at the hotel with visits to his mother every morning and evening, but Jo could not help noticing that when it came time for Ella's therapy, Daniel always seemed to be needed at the hotel. Gloria's visits had dwindled to one every three days or so, but Jazz showed up daily just before her grandmother was scheduled to begin her therapy.

"Come on, Grams," she would say as she wheeled Ella down to the rehabilitation center, "time for the torture chamber."

Ella would moan and then grin crookedly and shout, "Charge."

She spent most of her day in therapy—physical, occupational and speech—and Jo was relieved to see some definite signs of recovery after the first week, especially when it came to Ella's ability to communicate.

"Now, Mrs. Armstrong," the physical therapist warned Ella, "let's try that one more time. You need to show your daughter and granddaughter here who's the boss."

Jo started to correct the young man, but Jazz leapt in ahead of her. "Jo isn't my mom. She's my...friend."

"Our fliend," Ella added, still unable to fully manage the correct pronunciation of some words.

"Well, then you are mighty lucky," the therapist replied. "I wish all our patients had such dedicated friends. We might raise the bar on our rate of recovery."

In the evenings Jazz would regale Daniel with tales of Ella's progress. He showed the appropriate level of awe and respect in front of Ella and Jazz, but later as he and Jo walked back to the hotel, his mood shifted.

"Mom seems so fragile."

"That's because you're seeing her in the evenings after she's exhausted herself in therapy." They had reached the hotel, but Daniel didn't head for the door.

"Could we walk for a while?"

"Sure." Jo fell into step beside him as he turned the corner and headed toward the park. She was relieved that he'd elected to move away from the more lively section of the city—the theater district and Times Square. And yet his choice of direction set the tone for a serious conversation…one Jo had been dreading for days.

"You know there's no way she can ever go back to Star Pond," Daniel said quietly.

"No. I don't know that at all. And neither do you."

"Be reasonable, Jo. How will she manage the winter? And that doesn't even begin to address the routine details, like preparing a meal, taking a shower, shopping."

"There are home-care aides who can help with all of that and she's already used to them. They helped her while she was recovering from her hip fracture and she got along just fine."

"That was different."

"How?"

"It just was. Look, I don't want to fight about this. I need your support. Mom trusts you, and sometimes I think she believes that I'm only looking out for myself—doing what's best for me."

"Ella doesn't think that."

"How can you tell? Half the time I just nod and smile because I can't understand anything she's saying."

"Again, you just need to spend more time with her. When she's not worn out by all the therapy, her speech is fine. She's come a long way and it's only been a little over a week."

They walked along in silence for the next block.

"Want some coffee?" Daniel asked as they passed a café where patrons were seated outside enjoying the summer night.

"That would be nice."

"Can I ask you something?" Daniel said when the waiter had delivered their coffee.

"Of course."

"When your mother died and you realized that she wasn't…"

"Ever coming home?"

Daniel nodded. "If you don't want to talk about it, I understand."

"No. Actually, it helps. I think knowing Ella has had something to do with that. Being with your mother this summer has brought back so many of the good memories of my mom. Before the accident. Before she died."

"Mom would be pleased to know that."

"I've come to realize that it's not the dying that matters. It's the choices we make in life. I couldn't see that until I met Ella. Mom's death was so unfair—it felt intolerable to even think about life without her." She reached across the small table and covered his hand with hers. "But Daniel, Ella's situation is different. She's got time on her side, and you have the opportunity to make sure she spends it the way she wants."

He linked his fingers with hers and smiled. "I think the women in my life are ganging up on me here," he said.

"Gloria?"

"Not Gloria. She's getting restless again—the pattern is always the same with her. She swoops in and makes a big deal out of something and then loses interest. No. I'm talking about Mom and Jazz. I'm talking about you."

Jo swallowed hard and decided to ignore that last loaded comment. "How is Jazz ganging up on you? Seems to me she's matured enormously from the girl you first brought to the island."

"Yeah. Now she misses her friends on the island—especially Matt. No surprise there, but she has this harebrained idea that if she lived with her Grams, she could finish high school there—with Matt."

Jo laughed. "Yeah. She kind of mentioned that one or two dozen times."

"And what did you say?"

"What could I say?" *I'm not her mother,* she thought. "I told her summer romances could be difficult and if she and Matt were meant to be more than that, then it would happen whether or not she lived on Nantucket."

"No wonder she likes you so much," he muttered. "'Jo says…' and 'Jo thinks…'" he mimicked.

"Whoa. I have not given your daughter any advice. I have simply listened. Ella is the one encouraging her. I suspect she thinks that if Jazz came to live with her, it would help her in the quest to go home to Star Pond."

The waiter was hovering and people were waiting, so Daniel paid the bill and finished his coffee in a gulp. "So we're back to square one," he said as he took her elbow and escorted her through the close tables back to the street. "My head is spinning and you must be beat. What do you say we table this discussion for now and just enjoy the evening?"

"Sounds like a plan," Jo agreed.

"Ever take one of the carriage rides through the park?"

"No."

"Me, neither. Let's play tourists." He took her hand and jaywalked across the street to a line of horse-drawn carriages. "Choose," he said.

"It doesn't matter. That one." She pointed to a dapple-gray horse that had looked her way and whinnied. "He's calling our name."

The young driver helped Jo into the carriage, waited for Daniel to board and then climbed up to his perch. "No worries, folks," he said, showing them his MP3 player and earphones. "I drive. You talk—or whatever. I see and hear nothing." He tapped the reins lightly and the horse clopped into traffic.

Daniel wrapped his arm around Jo and she rested her head against his shoulder. "It's a beautiful city," she murmured, "especially at night."

"It can be overwhelming, though. I'm not sure it's the best place to raise a child."

Jo tilted her head so she could see his face. It was evident that he'd not yet let go of the discussion they'd had at the café. She couldn't help being touched that Daniel obviously felt comfortable sharing his worries with her. "Are you speaking in general or are we back to talking about Jazz?"

"A little of both. I won't deny that Jazz has changed since being on Nantucket. And for the better. She's more settled, more considerate of others, more curious about the world in general."

"And how is she here?"

"Bored, indifferent…. Not all the time, but when I think of her here that's the predominant picture. And the scariest thing is how easily she seems to fall back into that pattern when she's here. Sometimes I wish..." He paused and then shook off the thought. "But we were playing tourists. Now over there we have the famous Dakota building where John Lennon lived with Yoko, and then in the next block..."

Jo longed to smooth away the lines of worry etched into his forehead. "What do you wish?" she asked as she traced one deep furrow with her fingers.

He pulled her closer. "I wish I knew how to make sure Mom has the life she wants. I wish I knew how to give my daughter the foundation I had, the one I think you had. And I wish I'd met you sooner."

"I'm here now."

He traced along the curve of her cheek. "You are at that, but for how long? I can't ask you to put your life on hold for my mother or my daughter."

Ask me to put my life on hold for you as well as them, she wanted to say. "Daniel, I'm here because this is where I want to be."

"Because you've gotten so close to Ella and Jazz."

"Because I'm worried about you." There, she'd admitted it. She cradled his cheek with her palm. "So tell me what I can do for you."

He flashed the smile and made normal breathing a real challenge. "A hug might be a good start."

Jo grinned and wrapped both arms around him. "All better?"

"Like I said, it's a good start," Daniel said just before kissing her.

It was after eleven when they returned to the hotel. Daniel was immediately pulled into a discussion between an upset guest and the desk clerk. Jo took the elevator and chatted with Gus on her way to the penthouse. It was only when she was finally alone in the dark, impersonal room, facing the lights of the city's massive skyline, that she allowed herself to admit the thought that had been plaguing her all evening.

You are falling in love with Daniel. You can tell yourself that it's his connection to Ella and even to Jazz that keeps him constantly on your mind, but you know better.

It was true. When she had gone shopping she had looked at clothing with an eye to what might please Daniel. She had selected items she hoped would make him take notice, would not label her as the country girl she was. And the moment she heard his step outside Ella's door, heard him joking with the nurses, saw him coming her way, she felt the kind of pure joy she'd only read about in books before Daniel had come into her life.

Get real, she told herself. His life is here. Your life is…where? Not Nantucket. In just a couple of months the harvest would be complete and she would move on. She had deliberately chosen a career that would keep her on the move, not allow her to get too close to others. Friendships were fine, but something more? Something like what she was feeling for Daniel?

She clicked on lights and the television and went into the galley kitchen. She opened the refrigerator and stared at the contents—milk, fruit, juice. In the background the weatherman chattered on about the movements of the latest hurricane building strength in the Atlantic. Jo closed the refrigerator and gave the television her full attention.

Even if the hurricane was downgraded, a tropical storm that made its way up the coast, bringing with it unusually strong winds and rain, could mean trouble for the crop. It was way too early to predict the final path of the storm, but it would bear watching.

Jo flicked off the television and got ready for bed. But sleep was impossible.

I don't know what Your plan is here, Heavenly Father. Surely the idea that Daniel and I could ever build a future together is a pipe dream. This is no more than a summer romance, like Jazz and Matt, right? Guidance, please.

Suddenly Jo sat bolt upright in bed. The coming storm. Was that her signal to return to Nantucket? To get back to the business that had brought her to the island in the first place? Tomorrow she would go over the reports with Ella. Of course, the storm might just peter out before it reached them, but either way this was a critical time for the crop. Her place was there, not here. Ella would understand.

But the next day Ella was not at all happy when Jo told her she was planning to leave for Nantucket by the end of the week.

"Here," she said, banging her good hand against the arm of her wheelchair in frustration.

"But, Ella…"

Ella pointed toward her dresser. Jo scanned the items that covered the surface, trying to guess what Ella might want. "Your hairbrush?" Jo guessed, although she was sure Ella's mind was not on grooming at the moment.

"Vapers," Ella said, then shook her head and took her time pursing her lips the way the speech therapist had taught her. "P…p…papers," she managed.

Jo picked up a stack of colorful brochures and brought them to Ella. But Ella refused to touch them, motioning instead for Jo to look at them.

"Sunny Oaks," Jo read. "An assisted living community." She shuffled through the stack. Each brochure was an advertisement for a similar "community." "This one looks nice," she finished weakly, fully understanding Ella's dismay.

Ella's low growl left little doubt what she thought of the place.

"Daniel brought these?"

Ella nodded and her eyes filled with tears as she grasped Jo's hand. "No," she said as clearly as she had stated anything since the stroke. "No. No. No." Each declaration was accompanied by a forceful pound of her fist.

Jo caught the older woman's hand and held it, stroking her arthritic knuckles as she leaned in closer. "Ella, he's just looking into the possibilities. Nothing has been decided. But the stroke center here is temporary. You know that. The idea is to get you to a point where the therapists at a place like this can continue to work with you, continue to build your strength, and then…"

Ella drew in a deep breath and slumped back in her chair. She pulled her hand free of Jo's and waved her away, glaring up at her from beneath hooded eyes. "You p…p…promised," she managed, then closed her eyes.

Jo put the brochures back on the dresser and tiptoed from the room. Jazz and Daniel were coming down the hall and they were arguing.

"No," he said firmly.

"But why not? I can stay at Grams's and…" She spotted Jo. "He's impossible," she announced.

"Fathers often are," Jo replied with a smile. "Your grandmother is dozing but I'm sure she'd love to see you. I need to discuss something with your father, okay?"

"Whatever," Jazz said and strode down the hall in that hips-forward runway-model posture Jo had noticed the first time they'd met.

"I take it Jazz is angling to go to Nantucket?"

"It's not Nantucket—it's Matt. The kid could be at the North Pole and my daughter would see no reason she shouldn't hop a plane and go there."

"Maybe I can help."

Daniel's eyes sparkled with hope. "I'm listening."

"Well, I really should get back, and perhaps Jazz could come with me. She could stay at the cottage for a few days, see Matt and her other friends there and—"

"You're leaving?"

"Well, you don't have to make it sound like I'm deserting a sinking ship or something. There's a crop to be tended."

"Cranberries are the least of our worries," he said curtly. "I need you here." He sounded the way he had when they'd first met—as if he were her boss. So much for idealizing their relationship.

"And I don't work for you. I work for Ella. She hired me to do a job and I intend to do it. I am offering to take Jazz with me so you can give all of your attention to Ella." She let out an exasperated breath. "And speaking of that, what were you thinking? You just leave those facility brochures casually lying around when you know full well that…"

"What I know," Daniel began and then lowered his voice as a passing staff member glanced their way. "What I know is that the discharge planner has told me that they have done what they can for Mom here. Next step is a facility with a good rehab program where she can continue to work and hopefully continue to make progress."

"Have you toured any of those places?"

"I've been a little busy," he countered. "I had hoped you might go with me to have a look at them."

Jo decided to ignore that. "What if Ella wants to come home to Nantucket?"

Daniel's eyes widened and he actually laughed. "Are you living in a dream? Have you seen her? She can barely feed herself, never mind being able to dress herself or get to and from the bathroom without help."

"She had help before," Jo protested.

"She…" Daniel paused and looked down at Jo. "What's really going on here? Why are you running away?"

"I am not running away. There's a storm coming." She paused as the dual meaning of that sentence struck her. "Look, it's just that…" She swallowed the lump that suddenly filled her throat, and felt her eyes sting as she fought against her own weariness and guilt. "I promised her," she said finally.

"Oh, Jo, honey, we all promised her. We were scared and she was terrified and any of us would have said anything to help her through that, but we have to face reality."

"This wasn't some accidental platitude born of panic, Daniel. I promised to do whatever I could to insure she would not have to leave the farm."

"Okay, but now surely you can see that she can't possibly do that. You're the one who has been here for her therapy sessions, after all."

"And you haven't," she snapped. "Maybe if you had you would see that she's come a long way."

"But not far enough," he said, his mouth tightening into the same stubborn line Jo had observed on Jazz when the girl was not hearing what she wanted to hear.

"Look. You're right. This is none of my business. Ella hired me to do a job and I've allowed myself to become overly involved in the dynamics of your family. I apologize." She hitched her purse higher onto her shoulder. "I'm going back to the hotel. If I can get a flight out in the morning I'll stop by and let Ella know." She extended her arm for a handshake and he stood there looking down at her hand as if it were something foreign.

"And what about Jazz?"

Jo withdrew her hand. "My offer stands. If you want to let her come with me and stay in the cottage, fine. Anything else?"

"Yeah. What about us?"

There is no us, she thought.

"You've got a lot on your plate right now. Let's not complicate matters any more. Tell Ella I'll see her before I leave."

And like the coward she felt she was, Jo fled to join a throng of staff and visitors boarding a waiting elevator.

"Trouble in paradise, darling," she...
"Mom's sleeping..."

Chapter Fourteen

The last person Daniel needed to see at that moment was Gloria. But there she was, standing by the elevator as the doors slid shut, a bemused smile on her face.

"Trouble in paradise, darling?" She kissed his cheek.

"Mom's sleeping." Daniel led the way to Ella's room.

Gloria caught up with him. "I just stopped by to drop off a few things." She nodded toward the three shopping bags she carried and Daniel noted the names of three very expensive shops. "You do know that the farm girl is in love with you—or imagines she is. A little like Jazz's summer crush on that boy she's always talking about—Matthew?"

"Matt, and as usual you're imagining things."

"Oh, darling, do not sell me short when it comes to matters of the heart. It was obvious from the moment I met her. You do seem to have a way of capturing the hearts of women you meet on Nantucket," she teased.

"Jo is a friend. She and Mom have become quite close. Jazz likes her. I like her. Don't make a federal case out of thin air, Gloria."

"As our daughter might say, 'Whatever.' Ah, and look who's awake."

Daniel saw his mother cringe as Gloria presented her gifts, announcing each as if talking to a two-year-old. He couldn't help smiling when Jazz heaved a sigh of pure frustration and said, "Mother, Grams can hear and understand you. Stop talking baby talk to her and stop shouting."

Gloria glanced at Daniel and then back at Jazz. "Well, I see we're all in a lovely mood."

"Where's Jo?" Ella asked as she peered around Gloria toward the door.

"She went back to the hotel to take care of some things. She said she'd stop by later," Daniel explained. "Cyrus called."

"Did he say anything about Matt?" Jazz asked.

"We commiserated about the fact that both of us have teens who are moping around in spite of the fact they talk to each other several times a day." And before he could stop himself he added, "Jo's going back to check on the crop. How would you like to go with her?"

"Really, Danny, I hardly think…" Gloria began, but Jazz had already launched herself into Daniel's arms.

"Can I, Dad? For real?"

"I guess it would be all right as long as you don't expect Jo to wait on you. Remember she works for Grams, not you."

"I can help her. Matt and I can do the shopping and make supper and…"

"Just keep in mind that Matt also has a job—a job he needs for his college fund."

"Dad, I get it. Can I go? Really and truly?"

"Well, not right this minute, but yeah, check with Jo and see when she's flying out."

"I'd better phone her now," she replied, whipping out her cell and tapping in the hotel number. "Oh, these places never get any signal. I'll be downstairs, okay?"

And she was gone.

Daniel turned back to face two frowning women. "What?"

"I am her mother," Gloria huffed. "It would have been nice to discuss this."

"Jo's going?" Ella asked with a sigh of pure defeat.

Daniel knelt next to her chair. "Hey, I'm here. I'm not going anywhere until you're well enough to tell me to get a life."

Ella gave him a crooked smile and cupped his cheek with her good hand.

"Get a life" was an old joke between the two of them. When it had become apparent that his marriage to Gloria was falling apart, he had turned to Ella for counsel and advice.

"This is not the sort of thing you try to figure out on your own," she'd told him. "And I have no experience in such matters. If you and Gloria have grown so far apart that the two of you are heading off in opposite directions, then you get yourself to church and work this out with God."

"And what if God isn't listening?" he'd asked.

"God is always listening and He always answers. You might not be able to hear Him in that deafening city you choose to call home."

And now something in the way his mother was looking at him, something in the way she left her palm resting against his cheek, forcing his eyes to meet hers, told him she was recalling that same conversation.

Ella patted his cheek and nodded. "Get a life, son," she said, and her voice was as firm and clear as it had ever been before the stroke.

After Daniel left the hospital and made sure that Jazz intended to spend the remainder of the day with her mother, he went straight to the hotel penthouse.

Jo wasn't there. He tried her cell and it went straight to

voice mail. "James, have you seen Ms. Cooper?" he asked the desk clerk.

"She stopped by about half an hour ago and asked about checking out. I told her everything was covered and asked if I could get a car for her."

"And she said?"

"Turned down the offer of the car, then she thanked me and left."

Daniel's heart skipped a beat. Surely she wouldn't just take off. At the very least she would keep her promise to stop and see Ella before she left.

"She headed up toward the park," the bell captain reported. "Seemed a little distracted. I was worried something might have changed about your mother's condition."

"No. Mom's holding her own. Thanks."

Daniel walked quickly along the crowded street, and when he reach Columbus Circle he scanned the area for any sign of her. What had she been wearing? That green, gauzy top that made her eyes sparkle and a long, flowing skirt. He remembered because the first time he'd seen her wear that stylish outfit he'd realized he'd never seen her in anything but jeans before.

He caught a flash of green and dodged tourists and traffic to follow it. But it turned out to be an older woman in a green pantsuit, not Jo. Nothing like Jo.

Not sure of his next move, he shoved his hands into the pockets of his suit trousers and kept walking along the border of the park. He thought about calling Jazz to see if she'd connected with Jo, but abandoned that idea. Why raise questions—and Jazz was too much like her mother. She would have plenty of questions.

He was about to turn back when he saw her. She was sitting alone on a park bench under a canopy of chestnut trees. A slim book lay open on her lap and she was engrossed in writing something on the inside cover. He considered leaping the stone wall to reach her faster, but decided to take his time, gather his thoughts. Now that he'd found her, he wasn't sure what to say and he needed a moment to get his pounding heart under control.

"Hi," he said when he sat down at the opposite end of the bench.

She glanced up, perhaps expecting a stranger because her eyes widened. "Hi," she replied.

"Did Jazz reach you?"

"She did. I gave her the plane schedule."

"When do you leave?"

"We're booked on the six o'clock flight today. Jazz insisted on handling the details of getting us to the airport. She said something about Papa's driver."

"Her grandfather Barrington," Daniel explained. "What are you reading?"

"Emerson."

"May I see?"

She passed him the book and he opened it to the place marked by a satin ribbon. He read the words aloud.

"To appreciate beauty, to find the best in others, to leave the world a bit better…"

She joined him in quoting the rest. "Whether by a healthy child, a garden patch or a redeemed social condition. To know that even one life has breathed easier because you have lived. This is to have succeeded."

He passed the book back to her. "You don't seem the type to worry about success," he mused.

"You do." She handed him the book again. "Here. I bought it for you—as a sort of apology for earlier."

This time he opened the cover and silently read the inscription. *To Daniel, who has made many lives better…who has indeed succeeded. Jo.*

"Thank you."

"I mean it," she said. "Not just your mother's life or Jazz's. The way you treat the people who work for you is very special. You see them, remember them, take an interest in their lives and they feel better for it."

There didn't seem to be anything he could say to that, so instead he said only, "Stay."

She looked down at her hands folded in her lap and took a moment. "Do you know what a rescuer is, Daniel?"

"Probably not in the context you mean."

"A rescuer is someone who gets so wrapped up in the lives and problems of others that the outcome is more important to her than to the people involved."

"I don't understand."

"When I came to work for Ella, I was running away from my grief—from my guilt."

"What guilt?"

"The guilt I felt that my own mother had never had the chance to pursue her needs, her dreams. She spent her whole life living for the rest of us, making sure our dreams came true. We used to ask her about her dreams but she would just smile and say, 'Someday.' Well, someday never came for her."

"My guess is she did fulfill her dreams through you and your brothers."

"Perhaps. But when I met Ella and saw her determination to keep on doing the thing she and your father had loved their whole lives, I thought maybe this was God's way of giving me a second chance." She sighed wistfully. "I might not have been able to make Mama's dreams come true, but Ella was different. Her dreams were right there— in the soil, in that place, on that island."

"And she couldn't have done it without you—not this season. Not after the fall and now the stroke. You're going to give her what she could never have had on her own this season. How is that a bad thing?" he marveled.

"It's not—as long as I focus on that. Bringing in the crop, giving her what may be her last harvest."

"What are you getting at?" he asked.

"When Ella first asked me to help her stay put, I thought, 'She's strong and independent. She doesn't need me to stand up for her.' Then you arrived and suddenly I saw what she meant."

"Whatever you may believe, I only want what's best for my mother," he said in a strained voice.

"I realize that now—now that I know you better. But that first night at the hospital I thought all you wanted was to make things as convenient for yourself as possible."

"And now?"

"Now I'm beginning to see that you truly believe that it would be best for Ella to be closer to you. Some place where you can stop by and see her on a regular basis. A place where she can see Jazz—and even Gloria."

"Gloria?"

"In her way she cares very much for your mom. I think she's a little intimidated by Ella, but that's the very reason she respects and admires her."

"So, I don't understand. If you agree with me then why not stay and help Mom come to terms with the changes she'll need to face?"

"Because in spite of all rational thought to the contrary, I'm still on Ella's side. If she wants to live out her time at Star Pond, even if that means a shortened time, then she should. She's a practical and intelligent woman. She knows the risk she's taking. She knows the downside. But clearly for her the positives greatly outweigh the negatives."

"And your leaving helps how?"

"I am returning to the island to do the thing she hired

me to do—bring her cranberry crop to harvest. At least she'll know she doesn't have to worry about that while she focuses on convincing you and the doctors that her place is there on Star Pond, not in some fancy care center here." She took a breath and then continued, her voice just above a whisper. "I'm going because I have to start thinking about my future. I have allowed myself to become personally involved in Ella's life and yours, and in the temp business, that could be downright disastrous."

"Like it or not, Jo, you've become a part of all our lives."

"And that's lovely. I hadn't counted on the wonderful friendships that might be the perks of this. But the fact is that to grow the business, I need to get back to focusing on the task at hand—farming, raising a good crop, bringing in the harvest. And moving on."

"I thought we had… I thought…"

"We did. We do. It's been a wonderful summer, Daniel, on so many levels. We've both been blessed to have met and had this time together."

"You're breaking up with me?" He blurted out the first thought that came to mind and then smiled sheepishly at the ridiculousness of that statement. "That came out wrong."

"Maybe not. I was thinking that what you and I have shared this summer is not that different from what Jazz and Matt have shared. A summer romance isn't a bad thing, Daniel."

"And I'm not a teenager. I know the difference between infatuation and—" Love. He had almost said it and he saw that she was as surprised as he was. The result was a silence that stretched well beyond uncomfortable, as he traced the binding of the Emerson book and she studied her hands. Finally she stood.

"I have to pack and stop by to see Ella before I go." She

started along the path leading back to the traffic and racket of the city, then turned back. "We'll always be friends, Daniel. If you want."

"What do you want?"

She shrugged. "Still working on that one, but I could use a friend." She held out her hand to him and he took it and held on as together they walked back to the hotel.

It was amazing to Jo how easily Jazz had fallen back into her old lifestyle. In the car, she ignored the driver and took little notice of her surroundings as they drove through the city and out to La Guardia airport for the short flight to Nantucket. The mask of boredom and indifference Jo had noticed in those early days after Jazz's arrival on the island was firmly back in place. Her thumbs raced over the keypad of her phone as she sent text messages to her friends while listening to the throbbing beat of music she'd stored on her MP3 player.

Jo turned her attention to the driver. She learned that he had worked for the Barrington family for over twenty years, that he had arrived in the United States following the collapse of the Soviet empire, that he had a wife and four grown children—all of them college educated and pursuing successful careers.

"If you don't mind my asking," Jo said, "you must be near retirement age, Mr. Yenkovich."

The driver laughed. "I passed that landmark five years ago." He glanced in the rearview mirror and smiled. "So, you're thinking, why do I stay?"

Jo nodded.

"They need me. They trust me. I listen when they are in pain or when they are in joy. Finding work where you can make a difference in the lives of those around you isn't all that easy." He shrugged. "So I stay. And you? You run the farm for Mrs. Armstrong?"

"Yes."

He grinned. "See? You are needed as well. How would she have managed without you? And little miss there—you have done much for her this summer. She is different in a good way. Happier."

Jo had her doubts, as Jazz read some message that apparently upset her and furiously pounded out her reply. Then she ripped off her headset and turned to Jo as if they had been conversing the whole way. "Mother is impossible," she announced. "She's decreed that once Grams is settled in a good home, she wants me to come with her and Dad on a cruise over the holidays."

Daniel was planning a cruise? With Gloria?

"And what does your dad say?"

Jazz gave her that do-I-need-to-explain-everything-to-adults look. "He doesn't know, or at least I doubt he does. That's the way Mama operates. She'll put the entire plan in place and then casually mention it and Dad will say she never told him and she'll give him this blank look of surprise and say, 'But I'm sure I mentioned it.'"

"Well, it might not be a bad idea. Your father has been under a lot of stress lately, with everything that's happened this summer."

"She does this all the time. She gets this idea that we should play like we're a real family and then she gets bored and takes off."

"Maybe this is different."

"Please," Jazz huffed and crossed her arms tightly over her chest as she stared out the window.

But Jo noticed the way the girl's eyes brimmed with unshed tears, and the way her chin quivered as she tried to control her emotions.

"Hey," she said, pulling Jazz against her, "give it a chance. Sometimes when grown-ups are faced with the mortality of a loved one, they reevaluate their own lives. Maybe that's what your mother is doing. She loves and admires your grandmother very much." She felt Jazz's tears dampening her blouse.

"But what about you and Dad? I thought maybe the way things were going, maybe you and he might…"

"Your father and I are good friends and hopefully always will be, but this is your mother, Jazz."

The girl snuggled closer to her and heaved a sigh of exhaustion. "I just wish…" She shook off the thought, pushed herself upright and rummaged in her bag until she found her hairbrush. "There's our plane. I sent Matt a text to meet us at the airport." She was out of the car and striding across the tarmac to the small private jet almost before the car came to a full stop.

And suddenly Jo saw not Daniel's daughter, but herself. That same defensive posture. That same determination not to allow herself to be open to further pain and hurt. That same inner turbulence all dressed up in a costume of nonchalance and confidence.

Speaking of turbulence, Jo thought as she scanned the eastern skies, those clouds don't look friendly.

"Let's get going," the pilot shouted as if he'd read her thoughts.

Well, at least if rain was coming she wouldn't have to fire up the antiquated irrigation system, Jo thought as she ducked her head to board the small jet.

Surprisingly, the rain did not come, although the sky remained overcast for the next several days. The weather reports assured that rain was indeed coming, part of that tropical storm that fortunately had stalled off the coast. But Jo was unconvinced that they were out of harm's way and spent most of her days and part of the nights checking the bog and the sprinklers, making sure there were no leaks and no dry areas.

To her amazement every time she headed out to check, Jazz came with her. She didn't just offer. She was there. Of course, Matt and Cyrus also made regular trips to the farm to make sure Jo was all right and to offer their help. Afterward Cyrus and Jo would sit in the cottage's small kitchen, talking about crops and weather—and Ella. Matt and Jazz sat on the porch, rocking in the squeaky wooden swing, talking in low tones that were punctuated by bursts of laughter from time to time.

"Come on, Grampa, I'll take you home," Matt said one night, then turned to Jo. "I'd like to come back so Jazz and I can go into town. There's a bunch of kids gathering at the church for a sing-along."

"Sounds like fun," Jo said, and then realized the boy was asking her permission. "I… Sure."

Jazz beamed at her and raced off to the cottage's loft. "I'll just change," she called.

"Nothing fancy," Matt reminded her.

"I know—jeans."

"Maybe Jo would like to go along," Cyrus suggested.

"Sure," Matt replied, but his voice cracked and Jo understood that her tagging along was the last thing he wanted.

"Nope. I'm beat and I want to keep tabs on this storm. You go along. Just have Jazz home by eleven."

Matt's relief was evident in his broad smile. "Yes, ma'am. Thanks." He hustled Cyrus out the door. "Tell Jazz I'll be right back. Tell her to be ready," he added.

Jo chuckled. Jazz had kept Matt waiting on more than one occasion as she tried to decide on her wardrobe for the evening. "I'll tell her."

"I'm ready now," Jazz shouted as she ran down the loft stairs and out to the porch. "It looks like it's about to pour. Maybe I should come along in the truck and we can just go on to town from there?"

Matt held the car door open for her, waved to Jo and hopped in.

Jo was watching the weather channel, tracking the storm, when she heard the first splatter of raindrops on the roof of the cottage. She put her slicker around her shoulders and stepped out onto the porch, where she sat in the swing, watching the storm build.

At first the fat raindrops plopped onto the water-sealed railing of the porch, spreading slowly as they melted, one into the next. There was a distant rumble of thunder followed a minute later by a streak of lightning out beyond the bog. The rain came down harder until it was falling in sheets that obliterated everything beyond the edge of the porch.

Headlights hit the wall of water and Jo reached inside the cottage door for a spare slicker she could run out and give to Jazz. She was barely off the porch, dodging rapidly filling potholes when she realized the person emerging from the car was not Jazz.

It was Daniel.

Her heart leapt as she ran to him, threw the slicker around him and realized that she had missed him more than she had any right to.

"What are you doing here?" she shouted above the pounding storm.

He was grinning down at her, rain sluicing off his face as the wind blew the storm across the island. "...came to...should have told you..."

"What?"

"I love you," he shouted and for one split second the two

of them just stood there, thunder booming, lightning flashing as it split the night sky.

And then she felt the first solid pellet. It was staring to hail.

"No!" Jo shrieked and took off toward the bog.

Chapter Fifteen

Daniel's first thought was that she was rejecting his declaration of love. Then he realized why Jo had broken away from him. The ground was rapidly covering over with a thin layer of pea-size hail. He knew as well as Jo did that a hailstorm could virtually destroy an entire harvest in a matter of minutes. He pulled on the slicker she'd wrapped around his shoulders and took off after her.

When he reached the bog, he saw Jo still running. Up one dike and down the next until, exhausted, she stopped in the middle of the ten acres and bent double, her hands resting on her knees, her howl a protest against the already waning storm.

As suddenly as it had begun, the hailstorm was over. But the damage was done. As the last gasps of lightning flashed across the sky and the storm settled into a steady rainfall, he saw that the vines nearest him had been stripped bare of their berries. Berries that now lay like drops of blood on a bed of white pellets.

He slid down the side of a dike into the nearest bed to take a closer look. Maybe it wasn't as bad as it looked.

It was worse.

Not only had the storm stripped the berries from the vines, it had ripped off the uprights that bore the new growth for next season's crop. Insurance would pay for the damage to this crop, but next year?

What does next year matter? he wondered.

Daniel had always thought that this would be the last year for the bog. All Mother Nature had done was make that a certainty. So what's your problem? he asked himself. This is what you wanted—needed—to persuade Ella.

But Daniel felt such sorrow, such a sense of loss. He felt as if he'd been kicked in his stomach. He felt as if a part of who he was had been taken. He sank to his knees under the weight of his grief and let his tears mingle with the relentless rain.

"Dad?"

Daniel let the melting, icy pellets and berries he'd scooped up trickle back to the ground as he stood up. "Over here," he called, and saw Jazz and Matt hurrying toward him.

"How bad is it?" Matt asked as he offered Daniel a hand back up to the dike.

"I don't know. I stopped here. Jo's..." He motioned to where she had stopped and saw that she had retraced her steps.

"We'll have to flood the beds and skim off the destroyed fruit," she said.

"How bad is the damage?" Matt repeated.

Jo shrugged and took a moment to look out over the acreage. "Seventy-five—maybe eighty percent gone," she said, and her voice cracked.

"At least the insurance..." Daniel began.

"Ella didn't take insurance this year." Jo refused to look at him as she headed back toward the cottage.

Matt and Jazz looked to Daniel for direction. "There's

nothing we can do tonight," he said. "Might as well get some sleep."

"I'll round up a crew and be here first thing tomorrow," Matt promised.

Daniel nodded but he barely heard the boy. His attention was on Jo. She was striding back to the cottage, her posture so stiff and straight that she looked as if she were made of wood.

"Go on up to the house, honey," Daniel said. "I'll get your things from the cottage."

"Is Jo okay?"

"She will be," he assured her. "We're all going to be fine, Jazz. You go on, now. I'll be up in a little while."

But when he reached the cottage, Jo met him at the door. She was holding Jazz's carry-on bag. "I packed up her things from the bathroom, her nightclothes and laptop. She can get the rest tomorrow," she said.

Daniel studied her features under the low beam of the porch light. It was like looking into empty space. Her face betrayed no emotion, her normally lively and expressive eyes were clouded over.

"Jo?"

"Good night, Daniel. We'll talk tomorrow." She pressed the bag into his hands and closed the door.

Even as the light flicked off and he heard Matt drive away, he continued to stand there.

"Dad? Maybe if I stayed with Jo tonight?"

He handed Jazz her things. "Go on, now. Get some rest," he said. "Jo just needs some time."

Reluctantly, Jazz left and Daniel tapped lightly on the cottage door. "Jo?"

No answer, and yet he had the feeling she had heard him.

"You might as well open the door so we can talk about this." He waited. "I'm not leaving. I'll sit right here on this old, creaky swing until you let me in." He sat down and pushed off with one foot to set the swing in motion and make his point. He saw that the window was open, and kept talking. "Maybe in the light of day we'll see that it's not as bad as we think. I remember one time when I was about ten and we had a hailstorm, there was a lot of bruised fruit we could still salvage. It's not like Mom sells her berries to the fresh market from some roadside stand."

The complete stillness within the house told him she was there and she was listening so he kept talking. "Look, we've all been wondering how to work things out for the best. Maybe this is God's way of showing us a direction. Maybe…"

The door opened with a bang and Jo stepped onto the porch, her fists clenched, her feet bare. "Don't you dare make light of this, Daniel," she ordered, and he saw that her grief had evolved into the inevitable anger that comes with dealing with a disaster you did not cause and cannot fix.

"I'm not making light of it at all. I'm serious."

"You think God did this? You think He made Ella fall and then have the stroke and now this? What kind of God do you believe in?"

"A loving one," he replied. "Same God you and Mom believe in. Same one I hope Jazz has faith in. Why are you so angry? This wasn't anyone's fault. Certainly not yours. There was nothing you could have done."

"I promised Ella," she whispered and covered her face with both hands. "And we were almost there. Because she knew…she understood…"

Daniel was off the swing instantly. He pulled her stiff, unyielding form into his arms and held her until he felt the beginnings of her letting go. "Understood what?"

Jo sucked in a deep breath and raised her face to look up at him. "When I first came here and took the job, Ella told me that this might well be her last harvest. Not that she was planning that, but at her age she felt it was prudent to think of every season as potentially the last. She wanted it to be the best. I promised her it would be."

"But Mom knows…"

"I wanted this to make up for…" Jo said at the same moment.

"For what?"

She stilled and then shook off the question. "It doesn't matter." She pulled away and sat on the edge of the swing. "Tomorrow we'll flood the bog and get this cleaned up. Then we can see what's left to salvage."

"Then I'll wait to tell Mom. No sense coming at her with this on top of everything she's already dealing with until we know the whole story."

"How do you think she'll take it?"

Daniel sat down next to her. "Like she takes everything—in stride. Mom is amazingly resilient in the face of any calamity. I remember when Dad died, her sisters came rushing up here, making all sorts of plans to stay with her and eventually have her move closer to them. She was having none of that. 'Star Pond is our home,' she told them, and that pretty much ended any discussion."

"But now, with this on top of the stroke, how can she stay here?"

"She has me and she has Jazz. Surely between the three of us we can figure things out."

Jo leaned against him and rested her head on his shoulder. "And she has me—for as long as she needs me."

Daniel wrapped his arm around her and kissed her forehead. "That may be the best news she's going to hear."

In spite of Daniel's assurances, Jo could not seem to think about anything other than the ruined crop. Through the long night she would fall into an exhausted sleep, dreaming of Daniel's arms holding her, and then come awake. Wide-eyed, she thought of the unbelievable joy she'd felt when Daniel had announced, "I love you." And then, as suddenly, her spirits plummeted into the depths of the despair she'd felt when those drops of rain had frozen into pellets that stung her face and bounced off the surface of her slicker like so many marbles.

She lay there reliving the run for the bog, the race to will the damage undone. And finally the reality that not just this crop was ruined but probably next season's as well, and Ella had no way of recovering even a fraction of her losses. Jo willed herself to focus on those glorious, thrilling moments before the storm had come. He loved her.

But what does that mean? she wondered. What kind of life could we ever possibly share?

And once again joy would turn to sorrow. The storm had changed everything, although she was not at all clear how. It was a feeling—a certainty that whatever chance she and Daniel might have had had been destroyed by the hail.

Oh, dear Father, I don't understand what You want of me. I don't know how I can keep disappointing the people I care most about. How can I confess my love for Daniel when we have no future? How can I ever face Ella again? All she wanted was this one season—and if You were so inclined—perhaps more. But she would have settled for this one. Why take that from her?

Jo fought against her frustration and anger. The same anger she had felt when she realized her mother had died so needlessly.

"Don't think of this as the end, Jo," her father had counseled. "God has a plan for all our lives and you don't yet have the entire picture for what He has planned for yours."

Maybe Dad was right, God, but I have to say that I am

struggling mightily with finding some positive in all of this. I assume You had some solid reason for bringing Daniel into my life. Although I have to admit I don't understand Your purpose at all. He has a child who needs his guidance—not to mention an aging mother. Or what if it's not that You brought Daniel into my life but rather brought me to him? To help him with Ella and even Jazz, and that's the point? But then, why let me get all romantic and involved?

She squeezed her eyes closed and then opened them wide. *I could use some insight here. Please?*

Daniel tossed and turned in the single bed where he'd slept through all the years he'd spent on the island. He hoped Jo was getting some rest. He knew Jazz was sleeping because he'd checked on her twice now. Surrendering to his insomnia, he kicked off the covers and sat up.

The level of grief he was experiencing was so out of proportion to the events of the evening that he struggled to put it in perspective. Of course, part of it was the fact that he understood how this would hurt his mother. He hated that her dreams had been wiped out in five minutes of hail and wind. On the other hand, at least now he could put aside the guilt he felt every time he brought up the idea of assisted living. Every time, Ella looked at him with those eyes that were far more expressive than words could ever be. A look that said he was not only betraying her. He was betraying his heritage.

Is that it? he asked himself. Am I feeling this depth of depression because of the past? My childhood spent here on Star Pond?

Daniel walked to the narrow window. He stared out through the branches of the maple tree his father had planted when he was born. How many times as a teen he had climbed out this window and down that tree to hitch a ride into town to meet his friends after curfew. He smiled at the memory, for somehow his mother always knew but never said a word to his father. "You should take a nap," she'd say. "You were mighty restless last night."

Restless. That had been her code word to let him know he wasn't putting anything over on her.

And after he'd met Gloria, how often had he stood at this very window, imagining the life they would share? Coming here in every season—autumn for the harvest so his children understood his side of their heritage. Holidays and winter nights spent ice-skating on the frozen pond. And spring. There was no lovelier place on earth than Nantucket in the spring as its heavy, gray morning fogs gradually gave way to sunshine. An awakening.

Daniel saw the flicker of a light in the cottage and wondered if Jo was also struggling to sleep.

I love you.

The words had surprised him almost as much as they must have shocked her. And yet when he saw her running to him, the slicker in hand, her face wet with rain but alight with welcome, the words had come with such certainty that he would not have taken them back even if he could have.

And now?

Again that nagging feeling that somehow the storm had changed everything. Then, as if yet another bad omen, the light in the cottage went out.

Shortly after dawn Jo stood at the edge of a dike and studied the crop. She had hoped that with the coming of a new day, perhaps things would not be as bad as she had thought.

They were worse. With no more tears to shed, she sipped her coffee and stared dry-eyed at the devastation.

Then she dumped the last of her coffee on the soaked, sandy ground and headed for the farmhouse.

"Good morning," Daniel said, his eyes uncertain as he tried to read her mood. He looked like she felt. There were shadows of sleeplessness beneath his eyes and his forehead seemed permanently creased by worry lines. "How are you?" he added.

Jo shrugged and refilled her coffee mug from the pot on the counter. "Have you called the hospital?"

"Not yet."

Jo frowned. "She'll see the news, Daniel. You know how the media likes to play up any freak weather situation. By now somebody's probably posted pictures on the Internet."

"How can I tell her over the phone?"

"Then go back there and tell her, but do it today."

"Will you come with me?"

"I have work to do here. Somebody's got to clean up this mess. Hopefully we can salvage at least five or ten percent of the crop. At least I can give her that." She turned her back to him, unable to face him or her defeat.

After a long moment, Daniel cleared his throat. "Jo, last night before the storm came, did you hear what I said?"

"I heard."

"And?"

She whirled around. "Oh, Daniel, you don't even know what you're saying. You've gotten caught up in some whimsical summer romance—we both have. But it's not real. This…" She motioned out toward the bog. "This is real."

"Are you saying that you don't have feelings for me?"

"Of course I do. How could I not? You and Ella and Jazz have been…"

"I'm not talking about my mother or daughter at the moment. I'm asking about your feelings for me…for us."

I love you, she wanted to scream. Instead she turned to him and said, "There is no us, Daniel. We live in very different worlds. I will always treasure this summer and knowing you, but…"

"But what?" His voice was the one she'd heard him use when he was talking to a vendor who had not delivered what he expected.

"But other than a mutual admiration for one another, what do we really have in common, Daniel? My life is here—well, not here precisely, but with the land. The city is where you thrive. How can that work?"

He opened his mouth but nothing came out.

"And that doesn't even begin to address the fact that Jazz is part of you. What about her needs? Her life?"

"She likes you. You've made a real difference to her over just a few months. Think how you might impact her life if…"

"If what?" Jo forced herself to remain calm. She felt a little as if she were back on her high school debate team, assigned the task of arguing the exact opposite of what she truly believed. "We had this summer, Daniel. Up until last night it was a wonderful time for both of us. But summers end and it's time to move on."

"I told you I loved you last night," he reminded her.

"I heard you," she said, her voice softening to barely a whisper. And as if she had willed it, the phone rang, relieving her of the need to say more.

When Daniel didn't pick up, Jo reached for it.

"Leave it," he growled.

"What if it's the hospital?" Jo didn't wait for an answer, but lifted the receiver and handed it to him, as Jazz stumbled into the kitchen and slumped into a chair.

While Daniel held a terse conversation on the phone, Jo prepared Jazz a breakfast of toast, scrambled eggs and cocoa. All the while she listened to Daniel's end of the conversation. The caller was someone from the hospital. That much was evident.

"And you say she's had no television news this morning?"

Jo heard the garbled reply.

"But she's agitated? Not in pain?"

The voice on the other end became more impatient.

"What does her doctor advise?"

Short response.

"Well, try to calm her until you can reach him. Tell her I'm on my way. I'll get there as soon as I can."

He replaced the receiver and turned to face Jazz and Jo. "Mom's been trying to get out of bed all morning. She's determined to get up and go somewhere but won't give them any explanation."

He took out his cell and started punching in numbers. "Greg? It's Daniel. Have a car meet me at La Guardia at ten. What? Oh, yeah, I forgot. Well, make them as comfortable as possible—upgrade all the rooms and comp them some meals." He sighed wearily. "I'll get there as soon as I can, but I have to go to the hospital first."

"Daddy? Is Grams okay?" Jazz asked after he ended the call.

"I'm sure she is, honey. You know how she gets when there's unsettled weather within a fifty-mile radius. Her radar goes on high alert. I'm sure that's it."

"I'll come with you," Jazz said as she gobbled down the last of her eggs.

"No. Stay here and help Jo. I'll call you later."

This last comment was directed as much to Jo as it was to Jazz. Daniel kissed the top of his daughter's head, then squeezed Jo's hand as he headed out to the rental car.

As if her feet had a mind of their own, Jo followed him. "Daniel? She's a strong woman. Tell her the truth and she'll deal with it," she advised.

He nodded and then pulled her hard against him and hugged her as if he might never let her go. "I love you," he whispered against her temple. "I'm a grown man and I know real love when it hits me. If you love me, then we can make this work." He gave her another squeeze and then let her go.

As he drove away, Jo placed her fingertips to her lips and blew him a kiss, but he was already gone.

The best thing about the following week was that after long hours in the bog, Jo was exhausted and had little trouble falling into a dreamless sleep. Jazz had moved back into the cottage and had been surprisingly innovative in finding ways to make herself useful.

Rather than join the rest of the crew in the bog, she spent her time in her grandmother's kitchen, stirring up soups and casseroles from Ella's recipes. She made cornbread to go with chili. She tried her hand at roasting a turkey breast. She invented colorful salads from the bounty that neighbors and church members shared from their gardens. And when her first attempt at making a cake from scratch turned out to be more like pudding, she laughed it off, renaming the concoction her "volcano" cake.

Daniel called several times a day but most of his news came through Jazz. "Grams sent Dad to tour those assisted living places yesterday," she reported. "Dad says they are beyond awful—beautiful lobbies and public rooms to impress the families but behind the scenes? Not so great."

Then on the last day of the harvest to clear the bog of the fallen berries, Jo saw a strange car pull into the drive and watched as a man and woman mounted the porch steps at the farmhouse.

"I'll be right back," she told Matt as she waded through the flooded bog and climbed out. There was just something about the way the couple was dressed, the way they had looked around before going up to the door that made her uneasy. She was glad to see that Jazz had not allowed them inside the house, but had invited them to sit on the porch. She was coming across the yard toward Jo.

"Who are they?" Jo asked.

"A Mr. and Mrs. Waldon." Jazz handed Jo a business card. Waldon Estate Auctions.

"When somebody leaves an estate it means that person's died, right?" Jazz's voice quavered uncertainly.

"Oh, honey, not always. I'm sure there's a reasonable explanation for all of this," Jo said as she wrapped her arm around Jazz's shoulders and they headed back to the house.

Just then another car turned down the drive.

"Dad!" Jazz shouted and took off at a run. The couple on the porch stood up but waited where they were. Jo shaded her eyes with one hand as she tried to see Daniel through the tinted windows of the car. Another man dressed in scrubs got out of the backseat and opened the trunk. He took out a wheelchair and brought it around to the passenger side of the car and helped Ella into it as Daniel greeted Jazz with a hug. Jo's heart quickened. Surely if Ella had come home, everything was going to be all right.

"Ella," she called as she rushed to the older woman's side.

"Hello, dear. Jo, this is Howard. Daniel hired him to babysit me."

"Now, Miz Armstrong," the nurse said with a grin, "you know I just took this gig to get over here and see Nantucket." He grinned at Jo and shook hands with her. "Howie Johnstone. I feel like I know you. Miz Armstrong here and her son talked about you all the way here."

Jo felt a flush of pleasure and smiled. "Pleased to meet you, Howie."

"Well, let's get down to business," Ella instructed.

To Jo's horror, "business" turned out to be making the final plans for auctioning off the property and household goods. Ella had persuaded Daniel to let her stay on the island in return for her assurance that she would move to the assisted living facility in town.

"Why, that's wonderful," Jo said in spite of her struggle against the thought that Ella would end her days anywhere other than here at Star Pond.

"It's horrible," Jazz corrected. "Grams, you don't belong in some old people's home. You belong here and…"

"Oh, sweetheart, I had hoped that one day you'd come to love this place as much as I do—as your father once did. But we must be practical. With the crop destroyed and no insurance, my funds are quite limited." She looked determined to see this through. "I need the money from the sale of this place in order to live comfortably for whatever time I have left."

"Don't talk that way," Jazz protested. "You're young. People live into their nineties these days. You've got tons of time and…"

"And bills have to be paid," Ella said as she took the girl's hand with her one good hand and calmed her. "Under the circumstances I think I've come out of this pretty fortunate. Now, Daniel tells me you've turned into quite the little chef. How about putting together some snacks for us while we grown-ups talk business?"

While Jazz did as Ella asked, Jo sat in stunned silence as Mr. Waldon produced several copies of a contract and handed the papers to Ella to sign. She scribbled her name while Daniel held the papers for her and handed them back. In a matter of minutes it was over.

"We can hold the auction two weeks from Saturday,"

Mr. Waldon announced. "That gives us the time to advertise it and put together the catalog."

"We'll need to make an inventory of the household items and the machinery and such," Mrs. Waldon added.

"Jo can help you with that," Ella said. "Daniel, you and Jazz and Howard here can help me in the house, gathering the things I'll want to keep for the move into town."

Daniel nodded but could not seem to look at either his mother or Jo. "Come on," he said to the Waldons. "I'll show you around." And without waiting to see if they followed, he marched down the porch steps and started around the side of the house.

Chapter Sixteen

"Daniel, you need to get back to work," his mother observed one morning a couple of days later. "You're no good to me here and that phone of yours is buzzing constantly, and frankly it's getting on my nerves. Between Howard and Jo and Jazz, we have everything under control here, so just go before you lose your livelihood."

"Like I've lost mine" went unsaid.

In spite of the way Ella had attacked the job of sorting through decades of household items and memories, Daniel was not fooled. His mother's hollow eyes told the real story. She was driving herself too hard, determined to get this over with as soon as possible. Daily she assured him they had made the right decision—the best decision for everyone.

When he and Howard had taken her to the facility in town to register and see her one-room apartment there so she could decide what furnishings to bring along, she had smiled brightly and chirped incessantly about how lovely everything was. And it was nice—for someone else. But for his mother? He suddenly saw her stroke as a conviction and her sentence was to spend the rest of her days surrendering what was left of her independence to the well-meaning but paternalistic care of others.

There had to be another way.

"I can work from here," he said as his cell vibrated and he held it up as if to prove his point. It was Greg, reporting yet another half-dozen emergencies, most of which he'd been able to handle. But one in particular really needed Daniel's on-site attention.

"Go," Ella ordered as soon as he switched off the phone. "You can be down there this afternoon. And this time stay there until things are settled. Cyrus has already made all the arrangements for Matt and his friends to move my things to the home."

"It's not a home," Daniel protested, but Ella just lifted her good eyebrow. "Okay, but it's not a nursing home."

"I'll grant you that," she said and reached up to grasp his arm. "Danny, none of this is your fault. God has a plan for all our lives. Apparently this is His plan for me. I don't know why, but I suspect there's a good reason behind this move and I intend to open myself to that possibility."

Daniel stared down at her for a long moment. Jo had said something similar, but Daniel didn't get why God couldn't see that Ella belonged here, and let him and Jo build a life together. Wasn't that just as good as any plan He might have in mind for them?

"Stop questioning God's will and open your heart to the possibilities," Ella said as if he'd spoken aloud. "Howard! Daniel needs a ride to the airport."

Auction day dawned as gray and somber as the mood on the farm. Jo awoke with a start, her mind racing as she tried to fathom what she needed to do. But there was nothing to do. After today she would pack her things and take the ferry home. Hank had called her the night before to report that there was plenty for her to do once she returned. She suspected that he'd deliberately lined up extra work for the sole purpose of taking her mind off the disappointment she'd suffered here at Star Pond.

Outside her window she could hear the preparations for the auction. People were already beginning to arrive in order to have the first chance to preview the house and its contents. The Waldons had suggested selling the house and cottage intact rather than trying to auction the furnishings separately.

"Less morbid than watching the bits and pieces of your life held up for the highest bidder," Ella had commented.

"You don't need to watch at all," Daniel had reminded her.

He had returned the evening before in time for supper. The meal prepared by Jazz had been quiet and uncomfortable, with conversation coming in spurts rather than flowing normally.

"This chowder is as good as any I've ever tasted," Daniel had said and Jo, Howard and Ella had murmured their agreement.

"Is it too late for me to take that mirror?" Ella had asked after moments of silence. "It would fit well by the door of my apartment."

"I'm sure we can arrange for that," Jo had assured her.

And so it had gone. They had endured the meal like mourners gathered at a wake. Finally, as if she'd suddenly become aware of the morbid atmosphere, Ella had brightened. "I have an idea. Suppose we play a game of charades for old times' sake. Remember, Daniel, how your father loved the game?"

"I remember that he was terrible at it," Daniel had replied, but he'd smiled for the first time all evening.

"How do you play?" Jazz had asked.

Ella had been stunned. "Daniel Armstrong, do you mean

to tell me you never taught this child the game?" And without waiting for an answer she had quickly explained the rules.

"Could I call Matt and invite him over?"

"Absolutely, and tell him to bring Cyrus along. We old fogies will show you young pips a thing or two."

Ella's high spirits had been contagious, and within the hour the farmhouse had been full of laughter and good-natured joking. For a couple of hours everyone had put all thought of what the next day would bring out of mind.

Jo blinked back tears as she remembered Ella's peals of laughter as Cyrus Banks had tried to act out the movie title *High Noon*.

Later, when Daniel had walked her back to the cottage, they'd had the strangest conversation.

"I need to know something," he'd said. "The night of the storm when I told you I loved you, did you believe me?"

"I didn't know what to believe," Jo had admitted. "And then the storm came up so suddenly and was so devastating and..."

"If I told you now, would you believe me?"

"It's not a matter of belief, Daniel. We've been all through this."

"Do you care for me at all—more than just a friendship? Could you see us together?"

She had thought of little else for weeks now. In New York she had fantasized about them spending their lives together, but she was a practical person. She understood the realities of life all too well. It would never work.

"Daniel, you've made a life for yourself in the city. Your work is important to you—the way you've taken that hotel and turned it into a success—that's part of who you are, what you need to be happy. Work that is meaningful and productive. I guess in a way we have that in common. The problem is that our work is so different."

"Not really. If you think about it, I took an old, run-down hotel from my father-in-law and nurtured it back to life until now it's starting to produce a profit. How's that different from what you did here, taking Mom's bog and bringing it to life?"

"It's still different—you 'grow' a business while I grow a crop. City versus farm." She had shifted her upturned hands as if balancing a scale.

"Humor me. Pretend for one moment that there were no barriers to our sharing a life."

"Oh, Daniel, there's more than our work. There's Jazz. There's Gloria. There's…"

"Jazz adores you, and what has Gloria got to do with any of this?"

"I think she may be regretting letting you go. The way she was at the hospital and when she came here."

Daniel's laughter had exploded. "Gloria left for Australia yesterday with her tennis pro. Maybe one day she'll find some peace and happiness in staying put, but not now and not with me." He exhaled deeply. "I won't say our marriage was a mistake. How could I when it produced Jazz? But we were young and impetuous and we each thought we knew best. Both our folks tried to warn us, but I thought her father didn't think I could ever amount to anything, and she thought my mother was too dependent on me."

"Ella? Ella is the most independent woman I have ever known," Jo had protested.

"Exactly. Like I said. We were young and stupid. Fortunately we woke up and realized we could either be miserable together and inflict that misery on Jazz, or we could go our separate ways, maintain a friendship and each be the kind of parent our daughter deserved."

Jo had been silent for a long moment. Finally, she had said, "Australia?" and giggled. "There's something about the image of Gloria in the outback that just doesn't quite compute."

Daniel had chuckled. "I doubt she'll get much farther afield than Sydney, but the trip required an entire new wardrobe and Gloria is never happier than when she's spending money."

They had gotten off the subject and Jo couldn't help being relieved. One more minute and she might have flung herself at him and declared her love for him, begged him not to go back to New York, assured him that he could be happy farming the land—this land.

But Daniel wasn't going to let her off the hook. "I've been doing a lot of soul-searching these last few weeks, Jo," he had said. "Whatever happens tomorrow, I'm asking that you stick around after the auction."

"Well, I'm not going to just run off without saying goodbye. I want to be sure that Ella's settled and that…"

"Stop pretending this is about Mom—or Jazz. It's about us and how we're going to work out a life together." He had paused and looked down at her, his eyes suddenly filled with fear. "I mean, you do want a life together, right?"

"Oh, Daniel, we are very, very different people who lead very, very complicated lives and…"

"And," he had interrupted, "unless I miss my guess, we love each other very, very much."

"I know, but sometimes…"

"Do not tell me love is not enough. Do you love me?"

"I love you," she had admitted.

He had kissed her. "Then trust me to make this all work out."

"Jazz is right about one thing," Jo had said, still reeling from the kiss and the fact that she had just openly admitted her love for this man and the sky had not fallen. "You can be very bossy."

Daniel had grinned and given her another kiss. "Yeah, so I've been told. Might as well get used to it, lady." He had kissed her once more and then headed back toward the farmhouse. "Got people to see and calls to make. See you tomorrow," he had called.

And the day after that and the day after that forever if you still want me, she had thought suddenly. They have flower shops in New York City and public gardens. I can find work there. And in that moment she had understood that whatever it took, she would follow this man to the ends of the earth if he asked her.

By midmorning it was clear that most of those who walked the grounds and wandered in and out of the house were not serious bidders. The farm would go to one of several unknown proxy bidders that Mrs. Waldon would place bids for.

So when the auction began at eleven, people stood around or sat on the few chairs that had been set up in the machine shed to watch the show. Jazz sat with Howard and Ella on the farmhouse porch. They had all tried to get Ella to go to town during the auction, or at least stay inside. But she had insisted on watching and listening, although she had stopped short of actually taking a seat inside the shed.

Jo watched from the back of the audience while Daniel paced the sidelines. Mr. Waldon began the auction by making the announcement that this was virtually a one-item auction—the land, the house, the outbuildings and the contents of all would be offered as one lot. In the event the price did not reach the reserve set by the family, then he would begin the process of breaking up the package, selling off the machinery first, followed by the house contents, the buildings and the land. Jo noticed that with this announcement several people headed over to the cashier to purchase a bidding paddle—just in case.

Satisfied that everyone understood the rules, Mr. Waldon called for the first bid. One paddle went up.

Cyrus?

Seeing that, a local developer raised the bid and the battle was on. Cyrus. Developer. Proxy. Until finally the developer dropped out. The price reached a million dollars and still Cyrus doggedly flashed his paddle, almost before Mrs. Waldon could check her computer and nod to her husband that one or more proxy bidders were still in the running.

As soon as Cyrus had first raised his paddle, Daniel had stopped pacing and stared at the older man. When Cyrus kept bidding, Daniel seemed as concerned as Jo was, so she moved around the gathering to where he stood.

"Do something," she urged him. "Cyrus is doing this for Ella. He can't afford what he's offering—not without selling off his place."

Daniel's mouth tightened and he edged along the row of people to where Cyrus sat. He leaned in and said something that made Cyrus's paddle waver just slightly, and then the older man lowered his paddle and placed it facedown on his lap.

Mr. Waldon announced the current bid that was now approaching five million dollars—a bargain for land on Nantucket. He scanned the crowd for any other bids, his eyes landing finally on his wife, who shook her head once. The gavel came down and to Jo it sounded like a gunshot.

"Sold." Mr. Waldon thanked everyone for coming, and the people began moving back out to the yard, covering themselves from the fine drizzle that had started at dawn and not let up.

Jo watched Daniel approach Mrs. Waldon. He seemed nervous, almost as if he were afraid of what the woman might tell him. But when she nodded her head and smiled, Daniel's handsome face split into a grin. He turned to Cyrus and gave him the thumbs-up sign, and now Cyrus was laughing and shaking his head. Daniel said something else to Mrs. Waldon and then headed at a run out the side door of the shed and up to the porch.

What on earth is going on? Jo wondered.

Jo worked her way through the people waiting out the rain in the doorway and bumped into Cyrus.

"Come on, Jo," he said with a grin. "You're not going to want to miss this." He took her arm and moved toward the farmhouse at a brisk gait Jo would never have expected of him.

"It's over, Mom," Daniel was saying as they reached the porch. He had pulled a rocker close to the swing where Jazz held on to Ella.

"How much?" Ella asked.

Daniel gave her the price and she blinked. "Is that enough?" she asked.

Daniel shrugged. "We can make it work if you're willing to take the cottage."

"Take it where?" Ella asked and she glanced up at Cyrus. "What are you grinning about, old man?" she huffed, then turned her attention back to Daniel. "What's going on?"

"It's a simple question. Are you willing to move out of the house here and live in the cottage?"

"You mean rent from the new owners?" The air went out of her. "You're telling me we can't afford the assisted living?"

Daniel took both her hands in his. "I bought Star Pond, Mom. And I'm asking if you'd like to stay here with me—and Jazz."

"Why can't she live here in her house, then?" Jazz

demanded at the same time that Ella said, "Oh, no, son. It's too much. You can't afford…"

"I sold the hotel back to Gloria's dad. I used the money to buy this place, although I have to tell you I paid more than I thought I'd need to, thanks to Cyrus here."

Ella's eyes filled with tears as she looked up at Cyrus. "Cyrus Banks, what were you thinking?"

"That we've been neighbors now for over fifty years. I don't have the time nor the patience to break in a bunch of city slickers who don't know squat about living on an island."

"Okay, I get it," Jazz said, "but I still don't see why Grams has to move down to the cottage."

Daniel stood up and put his arm around Jo. "Because I'm hoping to persuade Jo to marry me. I'm hoping that we can be a real family—a multigenerational family."

Jazz's eyes widened. "For real?"

"We've got some details to work out, but if that works for you and Mom and Jo, then yeah, for real."

"Daniel Armstrong," Ella protested, "if this is your idea of a proper proposal then I have failed miserably. Now you take that young woman for a walk and you do this thing properly, and don't you come crying to me when she turns you down as she has every right to do."

Jo could not recall a time when she'd been more embarrassed. She hated being the center of attention in any case, but now everyone's happiness seemed to hinge on her. Overwhelmed by the drama of the day, she muttered an apology and fled.

Chapter Seventeen

"Way to blow this, Dad," Jazz said as they watched Jo run past the cottage and on toward the pond. "Well, at least if we live here I won't have to go back to that boring school." Her smile brightened. "I have to call Matt. He is going to seriously freak," she said and hurried inside.

"Well, don't just stand there," Ella ordered. "Go after her and take this, since you seem to have overlooked several key details in putting this thing together." She pulled off the engagement ring she had worn for over fifty years and handed it to him. "Now go, and don't come back without her."

Daniel pocketed the ring and ran to catch up with Jo, slowing his step when he saw her standing by the pond, flinging stones across the surface. He picked up three flat stones and took a place on the bank a few feet away from her.

He skipped the first stone and it sank immediately sending ripples across the water. They mingled with the ripples she was creating with perfectly cast stones that skipped three times before sinking.

"I'm out of practice," he said.

No response.

"At skipping stones, not to mention at knowing how to properly romance a lady."

A fraction of a second's hesitation and then she skipped the next stone.

"You don't have to marry me," she said tightly. "You did a wonderful thing for Ella. Leave it at that."

"Can't."

"Why not?"

"I love you."

"You think you love me," she corrected.

"Nope. Pretty sure on that one. Of course, maybe I've overestimated your feelings for me."

Another stone cast, but no response.

"What are you going to do here? You're a workaholic. You'll be bored silly inside of a month, and with winter coming…"

"I was thinking about buying a little inn that's for sale over in 'Sconset. It's pretty run-down but it has a terrific history and the best view of the Atlantic on the entire island."

"Suddenly you have money to burn?"

He chuckled. "Well, I wasn't planning to burn it. But yeah. Property in midtown Manhattan commands a tidy sum, even when the buyer is your ex-father-in-law."

"You've got this all figured out."

"Not quite. There's one key element that's missing." He edged closer, tossed the rest of his stones into the water and got down on one knee. "Marry me, Jo. Stay here with me and with Jazz and Mom. I realized these last weeks that what I've been missing in my life is a sense of home. That's what I want for Jazz."

"But the city…"

"Will always be fun and exciting and, yes, from time to time I'll want to go there. But this is where I belong. I realized it the night of the storm." His eyes filled with emotion. "I should have seen that as a blessing. It was going to make convincing Mom to give up this place so much easier. But I was the one who couldn't let it go."

"Would you stay if I said no?"

Daniel swallowed hard to get his words past the turmoil that blocked his throat. "Yes, but…"

She placed her hands on the sides of his face. "I love you, Daniel. I know now that I have loved you since that night my truck broke down in town. But I never dared hope that…"

"Dare," he said and fished the ring from his pocket. "Please say yes," he whispered as he stood and took her hand in his, the ring poised to slide on to her finger.

She was looking at the ring, at his hands on hers, and he caught the glimmer of a smile.

"Yes," she murmured and slid her finger into the ring.

He'd been holding his breath and it came out now in a rush as he scooped her into his arms and shouted with joy.

"Put me down," she said, but she was laughing and clinging to him as if she would never let him go.

Jo had settled on a Thanksgiving wedding. Her mother's death had taught her at least one important lesson. Life was too short to spend months planning instead of living it to the fullest.

The weeks since the auction had gone by in a flash. Jazz was thriving in her new school, having made a host of friends, thanks to Matt. She'd been elected to the student council and taken a real interest in her studies for the first time ever. Ella continued to improve, although it was clear that she would never again be fully recovered. She occupied her days directing the refurbishing of the cottage, even going so far as to e-mail Gloria for advice on colors and patterns. Daniel bought the inn in 'Sconset and hired members of his staff from New York to help remodel the place, with the offer to stay on and run it once it reopened in the spring.

And having sold her share of the temp business to Hank's twin, Jo prepared the bog for the next season's crop, turning the disaster caused by the storm into the opportunity to plant several new hybrid vines that her former corporation wanted to test. The deal she made to turn the land into a research center came with one important bonus—crop insurance.

In spite of Jazz's protests, Jo had insisted on a simple ceremony on Thanksgiving morning in the church sanctuary, to be followed by a traditional Thanksgiving feast at the farm. But Daniel had persuaded her to focus on the ceremony and let him take care of the meal afterward.

When the day finally arrived, Jo awakened to the familiar sound of the foghorn in the distance. She stretched and smiled as she looked at her gown hanging on the back of the closet door. It was the dress her mother had worn on her wedding day.

"My wish for you," her father had said when he handed her the box, "is that you and Daniel find as much happiness in your life together as your mother and I did—whatever the time God may give you."

In the interest of keeping things simple, Jo had asked two of her sisters-in-law to serve as her bridesmaids and Jazz to be her maid of honor.

"For real?" the girl had said, her eyes luminous with excitement. A moment later she'd been paging through the stack of bridal magazines she'd collected for Jo to study, looking for the perfect maid of honor dress.

Ella, being a strict traditionalist, had insisted that Daniel stay the night before the wedding at the inn and come directly to the church. "It is bad luck to see the bride on the wedding day," she'd instructed.

But Daniel had called Jo several times the night before, and her phone was ringing as she packed up the gown and everything she would need to dress at the church.

"Hey, how about getting married today?" he said.

"I wish you'd called earlier. I've got plans already."

"To marry?"

"Well, yeah, this incredibly handsome New York tycoon just came along and swept me off my feet."

"So I guess you wouldn't change your mind and settle for a Nantucket inn owner who lives on a cranberry farm?"

"I do love cranberries," she mused. "Is there a pond?"

"Star Pond," he assured her. "Come on, dump the city slicker and marry me instead."

"Well, the truth is that I haven't seen that guy around for weeks now. Maybe he dumped me."

"Then he's an idiot. Look, you've got the dress, the church is booked, people are gathering. What do you say?"

"Throw in Thanksgiving dinner and you've got a deal," she said, laughing. "I am seriously starving and it's only nine-thirty."

Daniel laughed. "I know what you mean. I just went down to the kitchen here at the inn, and the cook threatened to throw me in the ocean if I so much as touched one of the pies he'd just taken from the oven."

"I love you," she said, as she had said a dozen times or more a day every day since he'd proposed.

"Forever and a day," he promised.

The church was decorated with dried blue-and-pink hydrangea blossoms, fresh white roses and candles. The bridesmaids wore blue, and Jazz wore a gown of pink silk and the lace-covered designer stilettos that Gloria had sent her.

Daniel blinked back tears as he watched his daughter come down the aisle. She looked like such a grown-up, and he realized that in the blink of an eye he would be walking her down the aisle for her wedding.

Greg, his best man—and the new manager of the inn—nudged him and nodded toward the rear of the church, where Jo's father was standing in the doorway. Max Cooper held out his hand and Jo stepped into the doorway beside him. Daniel stopped breathing for an instant.

The woman he'd first seen wearing jeans and a sweat-shirt was a vision in a floor-length gown of ivory silk jersey. The vintage gown skimmed the curves of her body, the neckline squared to the edges of her shoulders and melting into long, fitted sleeves. Her dark hair was styled in its usual pixie cut with a single cream-colored rose anchored over one ear.

"Who giveth this woman…" the minister intoned.

"Her late mother and I do," Max answered and placed his daughter's hand in Daniel's.

From the moment their hands connected, Daniel was oblivious to anything else in the ceremony. He went through his part by rote, all the while thinking how blessed he was to have found this woman. And when the music swelled into the triumphant recessional music, he kissed Jo and realized that during the entire service he had been silently praying, thanking God and asking His forgiveness for ever doubting that there was a plan at work here.

Outside, the carriage Daniel had hired to take them to the inn was waiting. Everyone else would be there long before they were, but he wanted them to have this time, these moments alone as they began their life together. Under the shower of cheers and birdseed, he helped his bride into the carriage, climbed in beside her and covered them both with the cranberry-colored fleece lap robe.

Then he tapped the driver on the shoulder and gave him a signal. The driver grinned and made a show of putting on a set of headphones before snapping the reins. The horse tossed his head and stepped out, as the guests continued to applaud and call for one more kiss.

Daniel was not about to disappoint them as he pulled Jo into his arms.

* * * * *

Dear Reader,

In working through the idea for HOME AT LAST I had the pleasure of meeting Lucille Yokell, director of sales and marketing for the Wellington Hotel in Manhattan. She gave me her time and a valuable behind-the-scenes look at managing a hotel in midtown. Then while writing HOME AT LAST I was so blessed to meet Susan Indermuehle and Maria and Bob Winter while on holiday in northern Wisconsin—another bastion of cranberry growing. They represent the current generation of a line of cranberry growers in Wisconsin going back several decades, and their contributions to the authenticity of this work cannot be underestimated. It was Bob who gave me a tour of his fields in summer and first gave me the idea for the climatic black moment of the story. And it was Sue who was my tutor as questions arose during the writing of the book—always responding to my e-mails within hours, if not minutes, and going the extra mile when she wanted to be sure of her answer. Sometimes the true fun of writing a story like this comes in the people you get to meet along the way!

The bog and Star Pond on Nantucket are purely fictional. The last two bogs on Nantucket today are owned, tended and harvested by the Nantucket Conservation Foundation, but I was fortunate enough to be there during harvest on an October afternoon. I hope you enjoyed "being there" as you read the story of Jo and Daniel. Please go to my Web site at www.booksbyanna.com to enter to win one of two beautiful "cranberry" gift baskets and share YOUR favorite cranberry recipe.

All the best to you and yours!

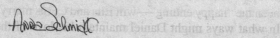

QUESTIONS FOR DISCUSSION

1. In what ways is Jo grieving for her mother?

2. How does the memory of her mother continue to influence Jo's actions through the book?

3. What role does Ella play in helping Jo get past her grief?

4. What do you think of Daniel's efforts to "care" for his mother throughout the book?

5. Is Jo running away when she comes to Nantucket? Why or why not?

6. How does Jo's faith manifest itself through her grief to help her toward the book's climax?

7. How does Jo's interaction with Jazz change throughout the book (and vice versa)?

8. What do you think of Daniel and Gloria as parents?

9. What role do you see Gloria playing in the family once Jo and Daniel are married and living in Nantucket?

10. Other than her infatuation with Matt, how does Nantucket influence Jazz?

11. Discuss what you think will happen now that there's been the "happy ending"—will Ella and Cyrus marry? In what ways might Daniel maintain his love of the

city life? Will Jazz be truly happy living on the island and attending the local high school?

12. How do you foresee the faith journey changing for Jo, Daniel and Jazz?

13. If Daniel had maintained an active church life in spite of his divorce and business problems, how might that have changed the story?

14. Do you believe that God has a plan for every life? If so, what "signs" did Jo and Daniel miss along the way as they struggled to find the right path?

15. In what ways was Jo's faith tested in the story, and how did she respond to each of those tests?

*A thrilling romance between a British nurse and an
American cowboy on the African plains.*

*Turn the page for a sneak preview of
THE MAVERICK'S BRIDE
by Catherine Palmer.
Available September 2009 from
Love Inspired® Historical.*

Adam hoisted himself onto the balcony, swinging one leg at a time over the rail. He hoped he hadn't been spotted by a compound guard.

But the sight of Emma Pickering peering out from behind the curtain put his concerns to rest. He had done the right thing.

"Good morning, Miss Pickering." He leaned against the white window frame.

"Mr. King." She was almost breathless. "I cannot speak with you."

"But I need to talk. Mind if I come inside?"

"Indeed, sir, you may not take another step! Are you mad?"

He couldn't hold back a grin. "No more than most. I figure anyone who would leave home and travel all the way to Africa has to be a little off-kilter."

"You refer to me, I suppose? I'll have you know I'm here for a very good reason."

"Railway inspection, is it? Or nursing?"

Emma looked even better than he had thought she might—and he had thought about her a lot.

"Speaking of nursing," he ventured.

"Mr. King, I have already told you I'm unavailable. Now please let yourself down by that…that rope thing, and—"

"My lasso?"

"You must go down again, sir. This is unseemly."

Emma was edgy this morning. Almost frightened. Different from the bold young woman he had met yesterday.

He couldn't let that concern him. Last night after he left the consulate, he had made up his mind to keep things strictly business with Emma Pickering.

"I'll leave after I've had my say," he told her. "This is important."

"Speak quickly, sir. My father must not find you here."

"With all due respect, Emma, do you think I'm concerned about what your father thinks?"

"You may not care, but I do. What do you want from me?"

"I need a nurse."

"A nurse? Are you ill?"

"Not for me. I have a friend—at my ranch."

Her eyes deepened in concern as she let the curtain drop a little. "What sort of illness does your friend have? Can you describe it?"

Adam looked away. How could he explain the situation without scaring her off?

"It's not an illness. It's more like…"

Searching for the right words, he turned back to Emma. But at the first full sight of her face, he reached through the open window and pulled the curtain out of her hands.

"Emma, what happened to you?" He caught her arm and drew her toward him. "Who did this?"

She raised her hand in a vain effort to cover her cheek and eye. "It's nothing," she protested, trying to back away. "Please, Mr. King, you must not…"

Even as she tried to speak, he stepped through the balcony door and gathered her into his arms. Brushing back the hair from her cheek, he noted the swelling and the darkening stain around it.

"Emma," he growled. "Who did this to you?"

She fell motionless, silent in his embrace. No wonder she had shied like a scared colt. She hadn't wanted him to know.

Torn with dismay that anyone would ever harm this beautiful woman, he felt an irresistible urge to kiss her.

"Emma, you have to tell me…." Realization flooded through him. A pompous, nattily dressed English railroad tycoon had struck his own daughter.

"Leave me, I beg you. You have no place here."

"Emma, wait. Listen to me." Adam caught her wrists and pulled her back toward him. He'd never been a man to think things through too carefully. He did what felt right.

"I want you to come with me," he told her. "I need your help. Let's go right now. Emma, I'll take care of you."

"I don't need anyone to take care of me," she shot back. "God is watching over me."

"Emma!" Both turned toward the open door where Emma's sister stood, eyes wide.

"Emma, go with him!" Cissy crossed the room toward them. "Run away with him, Emma. It's your chance to escape—to become a nurse, as you've always wanted. You'll be safe at last, and you can have your dream."

Emma turned back to Adam.

"Come on," he urged her. "Let's get moving."

* * * * *

Will Emma run away with Adam and finally realize her dreams of becoming a nurse?
Find out in THE MAVERICK'S BRIDE,
available in September 2009 only from
Love Inspired® Historical.

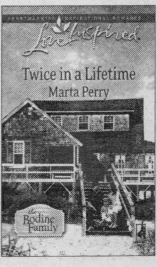

Brokenhearted
Georgia Lee Bodine
didn't want lawyer
Matthew Harper poking
around her family history,
even if that's why her
grandmother hired
him. Matthew's equally
damaged but caring heart
makes Georgia reconsider,
and open *her* heart to a
second chance at love.

Look for

Twice in a Lifetime
by
Marta Perry

*Available September 2009
wherever books are sold.*

Steeple
Hill®

LI87547

REQUEST YOUR FREE BOOKS!

2 FREE INSPIRATIONAL NOVELS PLUS 2 FREE MYSTERY GIFTS

Love Inspired®

YES! Please send me 2 FREE Love Inspired® novels and my 2 FREE mystery gifts (gifts are worth about $10). After receiving them, if I don't wish to receive any more books, I can return the shipping statement marked "cancel." If I don't cancel, I will receive 4 brand-new novels every month and be billed just $4.24 per book in the U.S. or $4.74 per book in Canada. That's a savings of over 20% off the cover price. It's quite a bargain! Shipping and handling is just 50¢ per book.* I understand that accepting the 2 free books and gifts places me under no obligation to buy anything. I can always return a shipment and cancel at any time. Even if I never buy another book, the two free books and gifts are mine to keep forever.

113 IDN EYK2   313 IDN EYLE

Name	(PLEASE PRINT)	
Address		Apt. #
City	State/Prov.	Zip/Postal Code

Signature (if under 18, a parent or guardian must sign)

Mail to Steeple Hill Reader Service:
IN U.S.A.: P.O. Box 1867, Buffalo, NY 14240-1867
IN CANADA: P.O. Box 609, Fort Erie, Ontario L2A 5X3

Not valid to current subscribers of Love Inspired books.

Want to try two free books from another series?
Call 1-800-873-8635 or visit www.morefreebooks.com

* Terms and prices subject to change without notice. Prices do not include applicable taxes. Sales tax applicable in N.Y. Canadian residents will be charged applicable provincial taxes and GST. Offer not valid in Quebec. This offer is limited to one order per household. All orders subject to approval. Credit or debit balances in a customer's account(s) may be offset by any other outstanding balance owed by or to the customer. Please allow 4 to 6 weeks for delivery. Offer available while quantities last.

Your Privacy: Steeple Hill Books is committed to protecting your privacy. Our Privacy Policy is available online at www.SteepleHill.com or upon request from the Reader Service. From time to time we make our lists of customers available to reputable third parties who may have a product or service of interest to you. If you would prefer we not share your name and address, please check here. ☐

LIREG09

Love Inspired

TITLES AVAILABLE NEXT MONTH

Available August 25, 2009

TWICE IN A LIFETIME by Marta Perry
The Bodine Family

Brokenhearted Georgia Lee Bodine didn't want lawyer Matthew Harper poking around her family history, even if that's why her grandmother hired him. Matthew's equally damaged but caring heart makes Georgia reconsider, and open _her_ heart to a second chance at love.

REKINDLED HEARTS by Brenda Minton
After the Storm

When a tornado traps Lexi Harmon and her ex-husband together, she prays they have a second chance. And as they work together to rebuild the town, she works on rebuilding their love—one piece of his heart at a time.

ANNA MEETS HER MATCH by Arlene James
Chatam House

Take one uncontrollable little girl. Add a home infested with bees. Toss in former childhood nemesis Anna Burdett, and what single dad Reeves Leland gets is one big headache! But could this reunion spark old memories and new possibilities for a future together?

DAD IN TRAINING by Gail Gaymer Martin

Special needs teacher Molly Manning thinks a dog is just what workaho Brent Runyan needs to reach his troubled nephew. After all, if Brent can open his heart to a loving canine, maybe he'll find room in it for Molly as well.

A TEXAS RANGER'S FAMILY by Mae Nunn

Home with the husband and child she abandoned years ago is the last place photographer Erin Grey wants to be. But Texas Ranger Daniel is ready to prove that her love is something he never gave up on.

HOMETOWN REUNION by Pam Andrews

Single father Scott Mara is busy renovating the town café. But Lori Raymond still remembers him as the high school bad boy who stole her heart. Can he show her that he may be a changed man but his love for Lori remains the same?

LICNMBPA0809